Also by Lloyd Ferriss

Secrets of a Mountain

Harry Stump: Maine's Psychic Sculptor

The Amethyst Stone

A NOVEL

Lloyd Ferriss

Acknowledgments

Thanks to Stephen King for his 1999 book, *On Writing*,
and to the late novelist Thomas Williams for his inspiration.

The Amethyst Stone
Copyright © 2014 Lloyd Ferriss
ISBN 978-1-63381-026-6

Cover painting and title page drawing by Jane Frost.

Designed and Produced by
Maine Authors Publishing
558 Main Street, Rockland, Maine 04841
www.maineauthorspublishing.com

For my wife, Jane,
with all my love

ONE

Climbing

March 12, 1953

A red pulse from the first warning light cast its flickering glow down the WGCM tower. What it revealed in midnight darkness pleased Paul, for the radio tower he'd studied from a half mile away appeared—close up—just as he'd imagined: three steel ladders welded edge to edge to form a triangle rising one hundred and seventy-five feet into the sky. The height was his father's guess, an answer to Paul's question a week earlier as they walked the access path east of Sylvan Road.

"Hundred and fifty. No. More likely one seventy-five," the boy recalled his dad saying, George Howland shading his eyes to better see the domed light at the tower's apex.

"Highest point in Crystal. Hell's bells, it's a third as high as Jayne's Hill. Tallest manmade structure on the Island is my guess."

Now, standing on the narrow cement base, Paul knew he wouldn't have to climb the way a lineman ascends a telephone pole, body leaning into space. Not at all. For the interior of the WGCM tower formed a three-sided tunnel of steel extending ladder-like into darkness. Grasping the first cold rung, he swung up and into the structure. It was easy. Right foot on one ladder, left on its opposite. Step once. Pause. Grasp the next rung and step again. The space formed by the grid-work was the perfect size, Paul thought. Perfect for an eleven-year-old. Climbing rapidly, he was proud. No matter that he was a sixth grader unable to read or kick a soccer ball to save his soul. He could climb.

His hands grew cold on the rungs. He'd expected that. It was March, after all, treetops dark and leafless below. He glanced at his fingers as he worked the rungs, his hands livid red in the first tower light now close above. And he remembered his mother's stove-burned hands. Her injuries. The ones that happened afternoons when she stumbled while reaching for a pot or fry pan at the back of the stove, her hand sliding over the burner. Paul forced the distracting memory from his mind. He didn't have to dwell on those things. Not anymore.

He passed the first light and in no time, it seemed, cleared the second. Far below, moving headlights defined a two-lane road. How surprising it was to see the cars but hear no engines; the only sound a low-pitched vibration from steel cables that ran skirt-like from tower to ground. *Guy* wires, his father called them. They hummed now because the wind was strong, and Paul realized he was cold. So cold that he found it hard to move his fingers—his hands grasping the rungs like crab claws, fingers barely able to flex and squeeze. Jab a claw to hook a metal rung. Step up. Disengage. Jab again. It was exhausting, and he wanted to rest. If he braced both legs against the tower, he could lean back in the triangle and warm his hands in his pockets. But planning the maneuver exhausted him. It was easier to keep going.

Sensing the nearness of the dome light, Paul was astonished to discover he was one yard short of a wood platform that capped the tower and supported the light above. Now he slumped against the metal rungs, looking up at the square platform and the pulse of light illuminating its edge. He was weary, his thoughts a jumble. Yet his plan was intact despite cold and his racing heart. He would carry it off. So he squeezed between rungs, turning as he did to lean out into the void—feet side by side on a rung, arms elbow-locked behind, hands grasping the tower. He'd done everything right. Nothing left except the letting go.

But he held on as he looked up and away, aware that he faced north because house lights scattered through the woods below ended at what looked like a great black pond. It was Long Island Sound. And he knew that faint star-like points resembling the Milky Way were villages in the Connecticut hills.

And something else: Green lights moving over the Sound defined a ship, most likely a ship going east to the ocean. How surprised Jenny would be to learn of his discoveries. Surprised and impressed. And there, looking north from outside the tower, one hundred and seventy-five feet above the earth, he imagined Jenny's face: her interested brown eyes and long braids, the wave of freckles over her nose. And his heart pounded so that he feared its thudding beat would throw him from the tower. His arms shook with the strain of clutching the tower rails behind, and he noticed for the first time that the rung under his sneakers was greasy— and he wondered why he'd failed to notice its slipperiness.

Instantly, the fatigue he'd felt moments before was erased by terror and, gripping the tower rail hard in one hand, he turned and slid to the safety of the inner triangle. For long minutes he remained motionless in the tower, feet braced on opposite rungs, hands thrust into the shallow pockets of his corduroy jacket. With eyes shut, Paul concentrated on warming his hands. Then—haltingly at first and with great care—he began the descent. And as his body limbered and the earth grew closer, he knew that despite discomfort and confused thought, he was skillful as an acrobat.

He passed the lowest set of lights and saw the tower's cement base. Half climbing and half falling through the last rungs, he landed in a patch of burdock that left thistly barbs in his clothes. Instead of pulling them out, he stumble-walked over stumps and brush to Sylvan Road. And as he neared home, he found that he was crying and wondered if it was because he'd come close to death or failed in what he'd set out to do. Overriding the thought was an immense desire for sleep. Reaching his driveway, he noticed—with relief—that the house was dark. Quietly, he climbed upstairs to his room.

*　　*　　*

"Get outta here."

Jenny looked at him, a smile on her lips, blue sneakers planted resolutely in the white pebble sand by the bus stop at Whitman Road. When he stared at her unflinching, she turned and looked at the tower, its red-painted rungs bright in morning sun.

"You lie," she said, brown eyes challenging. "You'd be flat dead on the ground if you did that. Or electrocuted like a squirrel."

It was after eight o'clock. In minutes their bus would pop over the rise on Whitman Road, brakes squeaking as it slowed for the Sylvan Road intersection. He had seconds to convince her.

So he spoke quickly, telling her how—from way up there—the beacon on Blue Water Light was small as a candle flame. He described the silent passage of cars on Whitman Road, the strumming sound of wind in the guy wires. And lights like stars in the Connecticut hills.

He broke off speaking when she looked again at the tower. Such wonderful braids, he thought. The two reaching almost to her waist, the end of each fastened with an elastic. One green, the other blue. It was as if Jenny's hair had a life of its own. Daydreaming now, he was caught off guard when she spun about and faced him, brown eyes filled with question and worry.

"You idiot. What did you go and do that for?"

"For fun."

It was the right answer. His inner voice approved. Don't tell anyone, it warned. Not now. Not tomorrow. Not ever.

Jenny had no time to question his response because the bus—yellow door open and red lights flashing—squeaked to its stop at Sylvan Road.

TWO

Elementary

March 13, 1953

Carpenters built Crystal Elementary School on Little Crystal Hill in 1927. That was the same year Rita Noble Hart graduated from Austin Teachers College in Texas and—determined to escape her monotonous upbringing in the Panhandle town of Vega—rode the steam trains north to Long Island. There she joined Crystal Elementary's young staff.

Tall and cheerful with fiery red hair, fellow teachers called her "Marigold."

Marigold preferred gifted children to the average run-of-the-mill sort, encouraging them in her sweet Panhandle accent to "reach for the stars." And Rita was recognized. Amid papers in her chipped oak desk was a letter clipped from the *Crystal Gazette* in 1934. Penned by the richest man in town, the letter by Alistair Campbell praised Miss Hart as "the standout young teacher who put my capable son on the road to Princeton."

But by 1953, nearly two decades after Alistair's letter, bad luck and loneliness had soured Rita Hart. Her 1938 marriage to Charley Lopper, a textbook salesman from Illinois, ended two years later when Charley disappeared with a sales clerk from Syosset. And Rita's salary was low—too low to buy a house or rent a good apartment. So it was fortunate for her when the school's music teacher, a heavyset woman with inherited money, rented her a cottage downhill from her own spacious place.

There Rita spent after-school hours with two orange cats and a martini. How many years had it been, she wondered, since anyone called her Marigold?

She was sick to death of Crystal Elementary and would flee the place in a heartbeat if it were possible. But she was forty-seven with eight years to go before she could escape to Texas with a pension. Teaching might be tolerable, she thought, if not for the two-acre barons who had moved from New York to the Island, where they spawned their unremarkable children. And now blacks spilling into her school from the shanties at Grant's Potato Farm.

*　*　*

From the second row, Paul heard Rita Hart's green shoes click their way across the floor. Stopping by her desk, she paused to count twenty-three children, while simultaneously releasing a cascade of three-ring binders—all landing edge to edge on her desk.

She looked angry. It didn't matter to Paul. He was too tired to care, exhausted from his climb the night before. Sunlight from a floor-to-ceiling window shone full upon his desk. A floor register added to the warmth.

"Good morning," Miss Hart said to her class. "I have bad news. Your grade-level test scores are awful. While a few of you excelled—and my congratulations to those who did—most of you barely achieved grade level. And as usual, we have four sixth graders unable to read."

Paul looked out the bright window. Below, three late-arrival boys crossed a soccer field, their heads appearing to float above their bodies. It was a mirage, he knew. Furnace heat coursing up the window distorted things.

Had last night been a dream? He fought sleep. It had to have been a dream. But no. His mind did not invent the cars that moved in silence, or green starboard lights on the ocean-bound barge.

In a final effort to stay awake, Paul concentrated on Miss Hart.

"The upshot of this misfortune," Rita Hart said, drawing three columns on the blackboard, "is that our class will divide into three ability groups: *Bluebirds* top. *Red Birds* middle. *Butterflies* bottom."

The blackboard blurred. He looked to the window. The split-neck walkers were gone. Goalposts swayed. And he was again on the tower, the dome light pulsing blood red. Time to squeeze through the tower rungs.

"Dumb ass. You snore. She seen you, too!"

It was David Kelly's hoarse whisper and David's elbow hitting his ribs.

"So let's get started," Rita Hart said, choosing to ignore the sleeper. The work before her was too important.

Beneath "Bluebirds" in column one, Miss Hart wrote nine names. Jenny was a Bluebird. So was Katherine Kimberly, a friend of Jenny's who lived in a large stucco house beyond the soccer field.

The ten Red Birds included Janet Woodbury, who raised her hand. When Miss Hart failed to recognize her, Janet wagged her fingers till she was called on.

"Janet?"

"You call the others Blue Birds, Miss Hart. Please make us Robins. Not just ordinary red birds."

Shrugging, Rita erased the name and wrote "Robins."

Then she put "Butterflies" on the board, her chalk breaking mid-word so she had to bend and retrieve the stubby piece from the white-dusted floor.

Below "Butterflies" went Paul's name followed by Owen James, Gloria Cantwell, and Brenda Long.

After recess and a school assembly, Rita Hart announced desk reorganization. Students in each ability group were told to buddy with a partner and move desks to the right chalk-mark on the floor.

Owen James, the best athlete at Crystal Elementary, chose Paul as desk mover.

"Old No-Hart's done it again," Owen said, as they slid the first of two desks into place. "What will that girl think of next?"

No-Hart was the sixth grade's nickname for Miss Hart, and had been since Jenny—bravely and recklessly—renamed her. It had happened last fall when their teacher, angered by David Kelly's donkey laugh, canceled recess for them all.

That was when Jenny raised her hand.

"Oh, Miss Hart," she'd said, her tone polite, "I do believe you have no heart."

Jenny was docked three recesses for the comment. When Paul asked what it was like alone for an hour with No-Hart, Jenny surprised him.

"Actually, she's not half bad when you get to know her," she said.

Reorganizing the room took fifteen minutes. When it was done, nine Bluebirds formed a circle next to their teacher's desk. Ten Robins laughed and chatted mid-room in their configuration. Four Butterflies had the north corner.

Brenda Long, a thin girl, hid behind her long straight hair. Gloria Cantwell sat between Brenda and Paul. Sixteen years old, Gloria wore the same stained dress every day. Owen was one of two blacks at Crystal Elementary. He was in love with Brenda Long, a fact he successfully hid from everyone but Brenda. She suspected and was secretly pleased.

Bluebirds and Robins had Rita's attention that day, but she did stop at the Butterfly circle to tell them about a new plan.

"We're going to learn grammar," she explained. "You'll learn the structure of language and in no time you'll be readers."

Her eyes drifted to Paul.

"No more in-class siestas for you, young man. What did you do last night? Watch Hopalong Cassidy reruns on *The Late Show*?"

She laughed.

*   *   *

Paul was first that afternoon to spot the round-topped yellow bus caroming down Wood Chuck Hollow Road on approach to Crystal Elementary. Minutes later he sat three seats behind the driver, watching black oak branches stream before the blue March sky.

"My dad's buying me an aquarium today," Jenny said as they walked down Sylvan Road. "He told me this morning. Just like that. Out of the blue. And it's not even my birthday."

They walked side by side. Occasionally their shoulders touched, his corduroy coat brushing her denim spring jacket.

"The aquarium's going to be ten, maybe fifteen gallons. My dad says it'll have an air stone and a pump to circulate water. Also a heater because my fish will be tropical."

They stopped by the edge of her driveway, a sweep of white pebbles through wild mountain laurel. Jenny, pensive all of a sudden, looked east down Sylvan Road where the WGCM tower rose above the oak forest.

"You're not going to climb that thing again, right?"

He told her he would not.

"Once is enough."

She turned and walked several feet toward her house, skipped once, then broke into a run—a girl in blue jeans, sneakers crunching driveway pebbles.

Paul watched from the road.

My friend, he thought. My companion in adventure.

*　　*　　*

As Paul turned from the Morans' drive and headed home, Lena Howland stood alone in her kitchen rubbing Unguentine ointment on her burned wrist. Papers lay strewn on the counter: a sheet of X-marked arithmetic problems, a copy of Paul's grade-level test, and a letter from Rita Hart in the same red ink that marked the arithmetic page.

On pushing open the kitchen door—just seconds before his mother turned and noticed him—Paul understood the story his scattered papers told. Miss Hart had mailed his failures home. Lena had responded by filling her glass with gin and water, the glass now empty by the plastic radio. The burn she was rubbing with salve had happened, Paul knew, when her hand grazed the red coils beneath a pot of furiously boiling potatoes.

She stared at him. Defiant. Angry. She knew he'd guessed everything—the boy was strange that way—and her anger ratcheted higher. How in hell had she, valedictorian of NYU class of 1935, and George, a Rhodes Scholar finalist, sired this kid?

Lena snatched Miss Hart's letter from the table and read aloud.

"He lives in a pipe dream, and I can't get through to him. Most of the others listen. He looks out a window. When the boys play soccer at recess, he stands watching. Or plays with the girls. The New York State Regents, the test that will determine his future, is two years away. We must build a fire under him, Lena."

She dropped the letter.

"What do you think, Paul?"

Her eyes went from his face to her glass by the radio. He knew she wanted to fill it up.

"May I go outside?"

"Outside? You can't ignore your responsibilities forever, Paul. Running off to Jenny's house seven days a week. Wandering through the woods looking at treetops. You think I don't see you out there?"

Again her eyes moved to the glass

"Oh, for God's sake, do what you want. Go out and play."

An hour later George's bullet-nosed Studebaker pulled into the drive. He changed into slacks and slippers, mixed martinis at the kitchen counter, and put them on the table.

Lena, clothes changed and wrist bandaged, lifted Rita Hart's oversized envelope and placed it between their drinks.

"There's something we need to talk about, George."

He looked tired. Pale. His body slumped in the vinyl chair.

"Please, not now. I realize it's important, Lena. But not now."

George was easily overwhelmed.

THREE

Backstory

1953—1910—1945

"Laugh? I howled!"

Standing in the dark hallway, Lena switched the heavy receiver from her left to her right hand. Her sister in Wisconsin seldom called, and Lena, oftentimes lonely, relished the chance to unburden through gossipy stories. "We'd just finished a couple of Consie's martinis out on her porch—it's actually warmed up in these godforsaken woods—when Consie made that comment about George wrinkling his nose as if he smelled something dead.

"What cracked me up, Greta, is that George screws his face up just like that when he thinks no one's looking. But Consie—the Constance Lyford I've told you about—was crouched in her bushes, unbeknownst to George, who was out for a walk. Raking away leaves is what Consie was doing."

Greta, a book illustrator, listened. Lena's marriage had gone sour; that was obvious. Still, the way she belittled her husband was unfair to George. He wasn't a bad sort, Greta thought. Too quiet, though. Troubled by the war, and Paul's problems.

George was a restless man. With spring days growing longer, he walked the half-mile Sylvan Road Circle twice after work. On weekends he loped along the gravel edge of Whitman Road, strides lengthening as miles went by. George did his thinking as he walked, wrinkling his face as he revisited memories. Like all men who reject the friendship of others,

George Howland's struggle to make sense of life was a solitary pursuit.

He was born in May of 1919, the son of Ron "Speedball" Howland, a pitcher for the Brooklyn Bridegrooms. His mother was Katherine Manet, a Canadian who left Ottawa to marry the pitcher she loved. George was born fifteen months later, followed by Marguerite in 1922. Unlike her serious older brother, Marguerite was an easygoing child with wide blue eyes and golden hair. A week before what would have been her fifth birthday, she died of spinal meningitis. The most vivid memory George had of Marguerite was a game they played days before her death.

They discovered a dead sparrow in a gutter near their Brooklyn brownstone and, with squealing laughter of children engaged in the absurd, gave the bird a funeral—Marguerite placing the sparrow on a moldy pillow she put on top of her head. Round and round the yard brother and sister marched. They tried to bury the sparrow, but the ground was hard. So they left it under a spindly lilac.

For years after the incident, memories of that morning haunted George. Was Marguerite taken because they sinned by making light of death? Or had spinal meningitis germs come from the sparrow she touched? Or from the moldy pillow he retrieved from the street and gave to his sister? He feared he was responsible for Marguerite's death.

For five melancholy years, George came home from school to find his mother crying. An overly protective woman, Katherine barred Ron Speedball Howland from teaching their son baseball.

"George could be hit in the head by one of your hardball pitches," she screamed at him. "Hasn't this family suffered enough?"

It was an interest in plants—roses in particular—that rescued George from the gloom of his parents' apartment. He was twelve when his jovial bachelor uncle took him to Brooklyn Botanical Gardens on a Sunday afternoon. There they had the good fortune to meet Dr. Eddie Waltz, a respected rose hybridizer in charge of the Botanical Garden collection. Alert to George's unexpected enthusiasm for roses, Dr. Waltz invited him back. Six years later Cornell University accepted George in its horticulture program. He'd excelled in math and psychics at Erasmus High School, where he also studied Latin and Greek. Though he had no friends other than kindly Dr. Waltz, he was happy with his career choice.

But the winter of 1937 was bitterly cold in Ithaca. On a blustery February night, forgetting his wool hat as he set off for the library, George returned with frostbite severe enough to cost him an earlobe. A month later, his agronomy professor tried to fondle him in the professor's own living room, where George had been invited to sample Dr. Thatcher's moonshine whiskey. George bolted out the door. But the incident, combined with frostbite and homesickness for his mother, prompted his decision to transfer to New York University. He would live at home.

The following September, an enthusiastic NYU advisor smiled as he reviewed the new transfer's record.

"A good set of grades you have there," he said. "You could major in horticulture. We have the program. But take my advice, Georgy boy, and switch to engineering. You'll make a lot more money than futzing around with plants."

George hesitated. He had liked Cornell's horticulture program before frostbite and Dr. Thatcher soured him on the place. But he was too influenced by authority to trust his compass. In later years he repeatedly relived—and regretted—his compliance in the advisor's office.

But two days after his unfortunate decision, life brightened when George met Lena Bieber in physics class. Their assigned seats were side by side. Lena's brown eyes, intent on equations Dr. Foote scratched onto his chalkboard, seemed to him a sign of intelligence. By the third week of class, they talked and laughed easily in the hallways.

The first time George took Lena to dinner, she ordered a martini. George did the same, despite instant dislike for its burning taste. But he stayed calm, and learned much about the woman with whom he was falling in love. Engineering was her major, chemistry her minor. Already accepted by the NYU Honor Society, she told him over a second martini that she intended to graduate first in their class.

Already thinking of marriage, George asked what she wanted to do after graduation.

"Be a top-level structural engineer," she said. "I'd like to work in Manhattan. Queens would be okay, too."

"But you're a girl."

George didn't notice her grimace, his eyes fixed instead on the near-empty martini glass Lena swirled in her right hand, green olive circling like refuse in a drain.

He learned that her parents had come from Germany to New York on the *Kaiser Wilhelm* in 1910, and that her father drove a trolley in Brooklyn seven days a week. Lena described a frightening folk tale her mother used to recite when she and Greta were young. And she told

George about a summer day in 1925 when the two sisters and a friend—roller skating hell-bent down 42nd Street—tripped and fell over a dead horse sprawled across the sidewalk.

Oblivious to the lighthearted tone of the story, George clasped her hand dramatically.

"Don't worry, dear," he said. "It's over now. You'll never live like that again."

For a second time that evening, Lena's expression darkened. It was fun, for God's sake, she thought, remembering the three of them collapsed in laughter while sitting in a row on the dead horse.

He wasn't like her. She knew that from the day they met. But he was her ticket to the middle class.

George and Lena graduated in 1940, Lena valedictorian, George a Rhodes Scholar runner-up.

In October they married at Grace Episcopal Church in Brooklyn. Hans Bieber, off work on a Saturday for the first time in seven years, looked elderly and frail in the pew, his handlebar mustache waxed for the occasion. Anna Bieber seemed worried. Greta the artist—flying in from Wisconsin that morning—enjoyed herself. Wearing a green Peter Pan dress and three-corner hat decorated with a feather, she patted Lena on the shoulder as her sister went down the aisle. Halfway through the long Episcopal service, she lit a cigarette in the church vestry.

"Your family made quite an impression," George told Lena as they danced at the reception. For an instant she hated him, but mellowed just as quickly. It's just George, she told herself. Things had, after all, gone swimmingly. George was a valued engineer at Grumman Aircraft in Beth Page, Long Island. The framework of their colonial in Crystal was already up. And Lena was pregnant, a fact she would share with her husband that night.

*　*　*

Fourteen months after their marriage, war changed everything. They learned of Pearl Harbor late on a Sunday afternoon. They'd gone walking on Sylvan Road, Lena pushing Paul in his blue carriage, and when they returned George turned on their living room radio, a four-foot-tall mahogany affair with a glowing orange dial. Roosevelt was speaking. The Day of Infamy.

George joined the Air Force. Two months into his tour, he was assigned to the Reno, Nevada, Air Force base for radio operator training in a Douglas DC-3. He learned quickly and, flying with his pilot and copilot on low-altitude flights over the Rockies, the three correctly guessed their future role in the war. They would "Fly the Hump," as the airmen called it, an exceedingly dangerous hop over the Himalayas from India to China. Their mission: to carry food and munitions to British and American forces cut off from overland supply routes by the Japanese.

Weeks later, they left Reno in a twin-engine C-47. After stops in Tennessee and Florida, they flew to eastern India via South America and Africa.

The first time George flew east over the Himalayas, he asked the copilot about shining wreckage on the sharp-topped peaks below.

"The aluminum trail," he replied, voice sounding weary in George's headset. "Remains of DC-3s and C-47s that took flak or hit weather en route home. Fifty percent chance we join them."

"Shut the fuck up, Herby," the pilot broke in. "You'll make our radio guy shit his pants."

Back in Crystal, Lena happily adapted to war. Hours after George's departure, she set out for Beth Page in their 1937 Ford, rehearsing the "hire-me" speech she planned to deliver at Grumman. As it turned out, convincing her all-male interview team was, as she later told Consie Lyford, "a piece of cake." Supervisors were thrilled to have a certified engineer when most of theirs were in Europe or the Pacific.

"You'll be in charge of the fuselage assembly line on the seven to midnight shift," the lead interviewer announced. "Can you start tonight?"

Lena nodded.

Consie became Paul's nighttime sitter. Millie, a 1940 Crystal High graduate, took care of him weekdays. That gave Lena time for sleep and afternoon walks. Her depression vanished. Except for a morning gin and tonic—sipped at sunrise before she slept—Lena all but quit alcohol.

She was popular, too.

Ted Andrews, a prewar employee too old for the draft, told his buddy that Lena was "his best boss ever, and a hell of a lot easier to look at than old George."

His comment found its way to Lena, who smiled.

✻　　✻　　✻

On the India side of his Himalayan run, George met Jim Evans. Their acquaintance began during a between-flight poker game in Karachi. Jim was copilot of a B-24 bomber targeting Japanese troops in Burma. Though in different Air Force units, both used the Karachi airbase.

A third player at the table that night was a braggart from the Tenth Air Force.

"The man is a horse's ass," Evans muttered in Latin, looking down at his cards.

Amazed to hear Latin in the Himalayas, George took his first careful look at Evans, a slightly built man with circles of fatigue beneath his brown eyes.

"So we have a scholar in this godforsaken hellhole," George replied.

At which point the Tenth Air Force braggart threw down his cards. "Educated fools," he said, toppling his chair as he stood.

For two months, George and the B-24 copilot got together whenever their down times coincided in Karachi. Twice they walked to bars in the poverty-stricken city a mile from the base, where they drank bad wine and laughed.

Jim was from Weston, Massachusetts. He'd majored in Latin at Harvard and, he told George, had a teaching job waiting for him at Lexington High School.

"But my interest—call it a passion—is sculpture. I work in wood. Small pieces, mostly."

With that he reached into the wide inside pocket of his airman's jacket, extracting a six-inch long sculpture of a pietà that he handed to George.

"It's crude, but what the hell. I carved it from Himalayan spruce with an Air Force jackknife."

George looked at the sculpture of Mary and infant Jesus, noting the expression on Mary's face and how the infant's eyes fixed on its mother.

"You religious?"

"No. I like to sculpt women. Children too. And animals."

Jim had a daughter, Emily, born July 5, 1941. "She's beautiful," Jim said, the fingers of his hands linked behind his head as he glanced at the bar's oily ceiling. "Blue eyes. Hair gold as an angel's."

Weeks later, again at the Indian bar, their second bottle of wine half empty, George talked about roses. He spoke quickly, afraid he would bore his friend. But when he saw Jim's intent expression, head angled to one side as he listened, his concern vanished. So George described the history of roses: how ancient Romans transplanted them from fields to gardens; how the species grew on every continent but Antarctica.

"Including this one," he said, stamping the floor. "It's called *Brunoni*, the climbing Himalayan Musk Rose. Its flowers are white. I'm going to plant one on Long Island."

"Jesus, that's fascinating," Jim replied, elbows planted on the table. "Here's an idea: after the war, when you have an extra Brunoni rose, mail one to Lexington. That's where Sarah and I are building. In return, I'll send you a sculpture in a package so small Lena will think it's a fruitcake. But trust me. It will be better than my jackknife-carved pietà."

✳   ✳   ✳

War went on over the high Himalayas. On a clear morning in March of 1945, the end of the long war in sight, the pilot of C-47 flight 232 taxied to the warmup circle in preparation for another supply flight over the hump to China. When he completed preflight checks and asked clearance for takeoff, the tower told him to hold for an incoming disabled bomber that had taken flak over Burma. When the plane came into sight, just two of its four props turning and smoke pouring from its damaged tail, George drew in his breath.

It was Jim's plane, the only B-24 in the fleet without camouflage, its tan and green coating removed to increase air speed.

Fragments of an Episcopal prayer came to George.

Have mercy upon this thy servant...

His pilot chanted, "Nose-up, nose-up. Now easy glide."

Seconds away from touchdown, both engines quit. The B-24 disappeared in a chasm short of the runway. The C-47 crew sat silent as black smoke obscured the sun. Minutes later a voice from the tower sounded in George's headset: "Flight 232 clear for takeoff."

✳   ✳   ✳

Five months later on an August afternoon, Lena waited at Crystal Depot for her husband's train, forehead pressed to the black steering wheel as she fought the effect of a gin and tonic. Grumman had fired her after V-J Day, her happy war years ended.

George, still in his Air Force uniform, stood in the first coach car. Through an open door, he looked past the coal car at the pounding engine. For years he'd dreamed of this moment. Now he didn't want to go home. If only he could ride to a different place.

FOUR

Amethyst

April 18, 1953

A Saturday afternoon. Warm for April. The sky cloudless.

They'd heard spring peepers the night before—tiny frogs Jenny called *Hylex crusifer*. Her plan was to hunt for them at McLean's Pond.

"Not to catch," she said. "They're too small. Too fragile to live in an aquarium. I just want to see one of them close up. Never have, though. They hide."

Paul needed permission before setting out. It was late to start an adventure, and they wouldn't be back until dark. So they headed down the driveway, still discussing frogs. The squeak of a metal wheelbarrow alerted them to George Howland at work in his hillside garden.

While Paul ran to the kitchen to find his mother, Jenny watched George planting roses. That very morning a United Postal Service driver had left seven boxes of dormant roses at the Howland address.

"Hard at work?" she asked.

Though not yet twelve, she had an easy way of talking with adults, and didn't hesitate to converse when a subject interested her.

George looked down from the hillside garden that was his memorial to Jim Evans.

"Not particularly hard," he answered. "Planting roses is my spring ritual."

She walked closer to where he'd set down the wheelbarrow.

"More of the white ones?" she asked. "My mom loves your roses. She plants them, too. Mom has three white ones like yours. Red ones, too. And others with yellow flowers. I don't remember the variety names. Anyway, my mom thinks your garden would be even prettier with more color."

When he turned toward her, she backed away.

His face was red. Cold hatred in his eyes.

"I plant *Rosa Brunoni*, the Himalayan rose. You're on my property, young lady, and what I choose to plant here is my business. You understand?"

"Of course. I only thought…"

Paul returned just then.

"Did you hear what he said to me?"

"Yes," he replied, quietly so his father wouldn't hear. "But don't worry about it. He never hits. Only talks. Best thing to do is steer clear. And never ask about roses."

Jenny turned and crossed the Howlands' lawn, Paul behind her. Through the forest they ran, hardly breaking stride as they dodged black birch and maples and skirted tall oaks.

Catching up with Jenny, Paul ran beside her, earth soft beneath his feet. They stopped at the height of land.

Below them at the bottom of the last wooded hill lay McLean's Farm, an expanse of green three-quarters of a mile wide. Gray split-rail fences ran through the new spring grass, creating pastures of varying size and shape. At the center of it all stood three immense barns, a white farmhouse to their left.

At a point where trees ended and the first McLean field began, an elliptical pond reflected blue. Paul heard his heart beat. And another sound: the shrill peep-peep chorus of *Hylex crusifer*. He looked at Jenny, seeing the trace of a smile on her lips, the freckles on the bridge of her nose. My friend, he thought.

That singular fact amazed him.

And he remembered how they'd met. They were five. It was the week before kindergarten. "Our new neighbors," he recalled his mother saying as they stood at the Morans' screen door. When Mrs. Moran ushered them in, he saw Jenny for the first time. She knelt on a bench at the kitchen table, drawing a dog in red crayon. When their eyes met she slid off the bench and kissed him full on the lips. Seconds later she was back at the table drawing.

"Why are you staring at me?"

The peepers went silent.

"You scared them," he said.

"Wait and see. They'll start up."

But they did not, despite Paul and Jenny's quiet descent to the pond and their leaf-by-leaf examination of alders that ringed its edge.

A faraway sound—hammer or hatchet striking wood—interrupted their quest. It came from the McLean barns.

Scrambling up the slippery north bank of the pond, they scanned the field before them. And there, standing in the distant farmyard, was a figure in white with an axe in her hands.

"It must be Mary McLean," Jenny said. "She's the only one left."

They watched as the old woman slowly raised her axe.

Then Jenny screamed.

"She's fallen! She's on the ground!"

And they ran toward the barns with long strides. As they drew closer, bittersweet vine obscured the crumpled figure. Then, climbing the last rail fence and crossing a red dirt yard, they stopped short in front of Mary McLean. She sat on an upturned log facing them, the same log she'd used minutes before to balance the sticks she'd split. A bruise ran across her forehead. A smudge of blood stained her hair.

She smiled.

"I tripped and hit this thing," she said, tapping the log with a bony finger. "Then a funny thing happened. As I lay there on the ground I heard angels in my hairpiece. It was sweet music. I wanted to stay and listen."

Her blue-veined hands brushed dust and wood chips from her dress.

"But I woke up," she said. "And here I am."

She tried to stand but couldn't.

Jenny moved close. "My dad's a doctor. He's home today. Is there a phone in your house?"

"Yes. But don't call. I'll do a jig to show you how healthy I am. Doctors get strange ideas, you know. Like taking an old lady's house."

Kneeling, Jenny wrapped her arm around the woman's bony shoulder.

"My dad would never take your house! Besides, we've got one already."

The old woman tugged at Jenny's pigtails.

"What's your name?"

She replied and introduced Paul.

"I'm Mary," she said, color returning to her face. "I'm alone now since Ross passed away."

"My mom told me. I'm sorry..."

Paul remembered Ross the milkman. His rusty blue truck used to stop at their house. That was when black-and-white cows had grazed the McLean pastures.

Now Ross was dead.

Mary looked at Paul. "Everyone dies," she said. "Me. You. That old Norway spruce next to my house. Death isn't something to be frightened of. I'm not."

It was quiet but for the *chip-chip* of English sparrows.

"I won't tell my dad," Jenny said. "What happened is our secret."

As Mary McLean rose unsteadily, Jenny rushed to brace herself against the woman's hip, her left arm around Mary's waist. How short the old woman was, Paul thought as he watched the two make their slow way to the farmhouse, Jenny's pigtails against the old woman's hair.

He leaned Mary's axe against the barn and, gathering kindling she'd split, carried it to the house.

The outside door opened to a pantry. A second door led to the kitchen. A single lightbulb hung on a cord from the ceiling. Below the light was a square table covered by a checkered cloth.

A refrigerator with a motor on top hummed in one corner. Opposite the refrigerator was a wood-burning range, its black firebox door bearing a silver cameo of a woman's face.

"Josephine," Mary said, noticing Paul's interest. "Napoleon's wife. Emperor Napoleon. Ross' father bought that range in 1880."

All of it was interesting: the silent house, the cameo-decorated stove, the smell of sour milk, and the aged woman. While Paul took in the atmosphere, Mary showed Jenny a vase of purple and yellow flowers.

"Johnny-jump-ups," she said. "Use your imagination and you see little faces. Already they're blooming in my garden."

They chatted until it grew dark.

"We have to go now, Mrs. McLean," Jenny said, checking her watch as she spoke.

"Call me Mary. But wait a moment! I have something for you, Jenny." Standing, she crossed the room to a china closet catty-corner between walls. Reaching for the highest shelf, she withdrew a purple-and-white gem. Less than an inch across, it was teardrop-shaped.

She put it in the girl's palm.

"My amethyst stone. Now yours."

"No," Jenny protested. "I can't—"

"Certainly you can. Let me tell you about this stone.

"In 1893 I lived with my father and sister, Miriam, at our old farm by Blue Water Harbor. That was the year my father took it into his head to visit the World's Fair—the big one in Chicago called the Columbian Exposition. Miriam and I ran the farm six days while Father was away. He returned on the seventh with two presents: a Columbian Wyandotte hen for Miriam, and the amethyst stone for me.

"'Father winked as he handed me the stone. He said it would bring luck. I thought he was joking. But that very week Ross McLean showed up at our house in his Sunday best and asked me to marry him. Of course I said yes. I'd loved Ross since schoolhouse days. But I thought he'd marry an in-town girl.

"Well, he brought me to this very farm that had one barn then and only three cleared acres. Ross was so very kind. And he worked so very hard. We wanted children but it never happened. Still, we had a wonderful life."

Jenny looked at her gift, turning it slowly in her hands.

"Thank you," she said. "I will treasure my amethyst stone."

As they were leaving, Jenny held the stone for Paul to see. Carefully then, she pressed it into the front pocket of her jeans.

They ran, waving once to Mary, who stood in the lighted doorway.

Despite the darkness, running was easy in the pasture, the new grass wet on their ankles. A full moon came out from the clouds as they neared the woods, making the path home easy to find. In minutes they reached the Howlands' lawn.

"I'm taking the Laurel Path home," Jenny said, referring to a trail they'd worn through a stand of laurel that separated their houses.

Her hand brushed Paul's shoulder.

"See you," she said.

FIVE

Camera

July 8, 1953

Blue Water Harbor. Was there a place more wonderful? Alone on the white-painted float, Paul was sure there was none. Cumulus clouds drifted in the north quadrant of sky over Long Island Sound. The tide ran high on the beach, pushing a green line of seaweed as it advanced on the brown sand.

In the way that a certain state of mind suggests its opposite, Paul thought about the long school year just ended. And it seemed odd to him—stretched out on the float in July—how summer vacation seemed to sneak up practically unnoticed. Winter was endless: floor registers pumping heat into the dry classroom day after day while clock hands crept nine to three. Then suddenly it was nearly summer, their room hot from sunshine beating on the flat tar roof, Miss Hart opening windows, wasps bumping clumsily against globe-shaped ceiling lights.

On graduation night, his class had performed *The Mikado*. Jenny was Yum-Yum in the operetta, her voice filling the auditorium as she sang:

I mean to rule the earth,
The sea and sky—
We really know our worth,
The sun and I!

25

Now Jenny was sunbathing on the shore, her red towel inches from the rising tide. It was noon, he guessed, his birthday party an hour away. Then—as if responding to his thought—Barbara Moran's Oldsmobile rolled to a stop on the gravel beach road. Paul dove from the float, swimming toward shore underwater until he could no longer hold his breath. When he surfaced, Jenny had sneakers in one hand, her towel in the other. Together they walked to the car.

"You haven't forgotten about my birthday, right? One-thirty like I told you?"

She slapped her head in mock exaggeration, dropping a sneaker in the process.

"I do not forget!"

*　*　*

At a quarter past one, Lena spread her green-checked tablecloth on the Adirondack table, straightening the cloth as she looked to the sky.

"Alto-cumulus and blue sky for your birthday, Paul. A fine day to turn twelve."

Leaning back in his wooden chair, arms wrapped about his knees, Paul followed his mother's gaze skyward.

When Lena sent him indoors for party plates and plastic forks, he returned to find Jenny in the closest Adirondack chair. She'd changed to a white blouse and blue denim jumper. Two rubber bands held her pigtails: one violet, one green.

"Happy birthday, Paul!"

She clapped her hands as she jumped from her chair, her eyes fixed on the table, where two presents stood beside Lena's double-layer chocolate cake.

"Why don't you open Jenny's first?" Lena said.

Paul grasped the two-foot-long present and swung it to his lap, bumping it accidentally on the Adirondack chair.

"Be careful!" Jenny cried. "It's fragile. If it breaks, it's ruined."

Paul sat still. With his left hand he gently brushed the top of the wrapped present, sensing a hollow beneath. And when he felt its smooth sides and metal edges, he knew it was an aquarium. He unwrapped it slowly and carefully, revealing its glass sides and slate bottom. There was a coil of plastic tubing and other accessories inside the tank.

Tired of his slow unwrapping, Jenny lifted the fish tank from his lap and placed it on the lawn.

"This is the air pump," she said, taking a turquoise cube from the tank. Working quickly, she attached the plastic tubing to the pump, linking it to a green oval disk.

"It's your air stone," she said. "You've seen the one in my aquarium. The pump forces air through the disk's porous stone and the bubbles look beautiful rising through the aquarium plants. These bubbles put some oxygen in the water. But most of the oxygen your fish will need enters at the top of an aquarium where water meets air."

From her yellow Adirondack chair, Lena studied Jenny. What a well-spoken child, she thought. The girl understands science. She completes sentences. Her eyes focus. How different she is from Paul! And she thought of her son, who often quit speaking in midsentence, as if losing his train of thought.

She wanted a drink, the need rising from deep within. Always at noon it began. One glass would ease her tension. But she wouldn't pour a drink. Certainly not today. Not in front of that smart girl.

To distract her thirst, Lena leaned forward to better observe. How close they knelt together on the lawn, she thought.

They had the pump and air stone assembled in the otherwise empty aquarium. From a cardboard bag, Paul poured white sand into the fish tank.

When he stood and lifted his second present from the table, tearing a strip of wrapping from the gift, Lena worried. Her present would not measure up to Jenny's gift. Not to Paul's mind. What had she been thinking? That her Kodak Box Brownie, now forty years old, would make a hit with the kid?

As a child she'd loved the camera, carrying it by its leather strap when she went with Greta to Prospect Park. That was where she had taken the picture of her sister standing on a branch high in a willow tree, Greta's hands outstretched for balance. Using the same camera, she had photographed her father, Hans Bieber, muscles flexed as he stood waist-deep in salt water at the beach on Coney Island. And where were the pictures now? Were they in her parents' attic? With her sister in Wisconsin? Lost? And she bowed her head, struck by the relentless passage of time.

Paul pulled the last ribbon from the camera. Lena watched him study the Box Brownie while turning it front and sideways in his hands.

He ran his fingers over the metal film advance knob. He looked into the viewfinder window, moving the camera in a slow arc as he did. And as Lena watched, she knew exactly what her son observed: a parade of trees flowing like motion pictures in the glass.

"It has film in it," she said. "I loaded your camera before wrapping it. You can take a picture anytime."

She saw him turn the camera toward Jenny. A second later, Lena wondered if her eyes were playing tricks. Had Paul moved the shutter so fast that Jenny didn't realize she'd been photographed?

Yes, he had!

"You can take twelve pictures on a roll," she said. "Eleven now. Always turn the knob after you take a picture. Look through the red circle as you turn, and stop when you see the next number. Then you're ready to make another exposure. Do that every time you take a photograph. You'll have a double exposure if you don't—that's a picture on top of a picture."

Paul met her eyes, his head angled to one side as he listened. He'd understood everything, she concluded. That—and his rare smile—made her very happy. So when he asked if they could skip dessert for now so he could take pictures at the McLean Farm, she nodded.

"Of course."

Lena watched the children pass the Himalayan roses, Paul holding the Kodak Box Brownie by its leather strap. In the green woods cicadas sang. Above her, clouds banked layer upon layer. Crystal was a beautiful place, she thought. Clean. Much cleaner than the city. How lucky they were!

But her happiness didn't last. Paul was, after all, woefully behind his class. And she was bored. Bored and frightened that she couldn't deny her thirst early in the day.

Lena went indoors. There were kitchen chores to do, she reasoned, a cake to cover and ice cream to put in the freezer.

SIX

Composition

July 8, 1953
Afternoon

Jenny ran far ahead as they crossed the woods to Mary's farm. Paul, determined to protect his camera from every briar and sapling, nearly lost sight of her.

"Wait up!" he yelled.

She did. But again he lagged. Then he stopped altogether on the height of land above the farm's pond. Jenny continued to the fence that separated woods from pasture. There she climbed to the top split rail and sat looking back at Paul, motionless amid the trees.

He's entranced by the camera, she thought. That was okay with her. The fence rail made a comfortable seat. It was pleasantly cool in the shade—trees on one side, the farm on the other. Reaching into the pocket of her denim dress, she felt the amethyst stone. It was safe.

From the hillside, Paul studied Mary's farm in the camera viewfinder.

It was like a magic window, he thought. Hold the camera just so and the window removed everything he did not want to have in his picture: cars on the Whitman Road, a junked Model-A Ford in the left pasture, the WGCM radio tower. But straight ahead was the heart of Mary's farm: the ellipse-shaped pond, a honey locust tree at its edge and distant barns gray against the sky.

Moving the camera ever so slightly left, Paul brought into his composition two nearby trees that framed the scene. He moved the shutter and heard its tiny click.

Recalling his mother's instruction, he turned the film advance knob until the number three appeared within a red circle.

"Are you going to stand there all day?" Jenny called. "It's your new camera and all, but holy cow! How long does it take to take one picture?"

They crossed the fence together and Jenny headed for the pond. She had with her a paper birthday cup to catch pinhead-size water bugs they'd discovered on their last visit. Uninterested, Paul crossed the first field to a garage-size boulder Jenny called "a glacial erratic." He had the image in the camera viewfinder when Jenny interrupted.

"What's so great about a rock?"

He shrugged.

"It's big."

"You could find something more interesting."

"Like what?"

"Like me."

So he took her picture standing, hands on her hips, on top of the rock.

"God, it's high up here! Stand back. I'm jumping."

His second photo of Jenny had her sitting in the green pasture grass, her skirt fanned out in a perfect circle. At her suggestion, she held a bouquet of Indian paintbrush flowers. His third and final picture was a close-up of Jenny's face, so close, in fact, that he saw her freckles in his viewfinder.

Jenny suggested they visit Mary. "It's been forever since we've seen her and I hope she's not mad. I mean, after giving me the amethyst stone and all."

When they reached the barns and crossed the dusty farmyard, they spotted Mary pulling weeds from her flower garden. Unaware of their approach, the elderly woman continued weeding until Jenny brushed her sneaker on the sun-baked earth in an attempt to get Mary's attention without startling her.

It worked.

"What a treat!" the elderly woman exclaimed. "I've been thinking about you two, out of school now and enjoying summer. Having a good time of it, I imagine?"

Mary hugged Jenny, gently pulled her pigtails, and talked about the garden.

"It's smaller than it used to be," she said. "I had fifteen kinds of flowers growing here at one time. This year I planted seed for just two kinds: sweet pea and brown-eyed Susan. My favorites, as you might guess."

They sat together on rusty lawn chairs. Mary had grown frail in the months since their last visit. And she seemed nervous, her hands moving distractedly in her lap. It wasn't long before she revealed the source of her agitation.

"My nephew Jack—that's Jack Tainter, my sister Miriam's youngest—showed up here last week in a shiny black car. With him were three men in brown suits and pink ties. They followed Jack into the first field, where he stood like a man about town swinging his arms and puffing out his chest.

"Now I wasn't born yesterday. I know what Jack's about. I've willed him the farm, and here he is showing my place to city slickers under my very nose. So I telephoned him after.

"'Jack,' I said, 'those two you brought out here—they don't look like farmers to me.'"

"'They ain't, Mary,' he tells me. 'Them are real estate developers, and believe you me, they want those acres for house lots. Nobody in Crystal keeps cows nowadays. You and Ross were the last.'"

Pushing herself up and out of the lawn chair, Mary walked slowly to the center of her red dirt farmyard. There she stood gazing at the largest of her three barns. Paul followed.

"Of course, he can't sell anything until I'm gone," she said. "But it pains me to know that the farm Ross made beautiful is going to be ruined. Ross built this big barn in nineteen fifteen. We had cows in every stanchion until five years ago. Now it's empty but for sparrows."

Paul photographed her so close that he saw the lines of her face in his viewfinder, the peaked roof of the broad barn behind her.

Jenny ran to Mary, hugging her as she glared at Paul.

"Impolite," she hissed.

Next day, Lena brought Paul's film to Dr. Albert's Pharmacy at the corner of Main Street and New York Avenue in Crystal. Three weeks later, old Mr. Kemper, who ran the store for Dr. Albert, called to say the prints were ready. Lena drove the Studebaker to Crystal, Paul silent beside her as he watched branches stream past the window.

Ten minutes later, they stood at the film counter, stepping to one side so portly Mr. Kemper had room to squeeze between the glass cabinets that formed his film counter.

"Space gets smaller all the time," he muttered.

From a cubbyhole behind him, Mr. Kemper retrieved a yellow-and-black envelope.

"Been a few weeks," he said, handing the envelope to Paul. "Then again, your film traveled round trip from here to Eastman and Kodak out in Rochester."

The old man leaned close as Paul pulled photographs from the envelope and arranged them in a line on the counter.

"You photographed the sun in this one," the old man said, tapping a picture of what appeared to be a white ball, the only recognizable object a sneaker-clad foot at the lower right.

"This next one's no good neither," he went on. "Blurry. Too close to your subject."

More than half the pictures were failures. Camera shake accounted for blurred images. A tilted horizon line spoiled a couple of others. And he'd pointed his camera too low for what might have been a good picture of Jenny on the glacial erratic.

"Cut off your girlfriend's head in this one," Mr. Kemper said, stifling a giggle when he caught Lena's cold stare.

They were a disappointing bunch of pictures, Paul thought. Before the trip to Dr. Albert's Pharmacy, Paul thought his pictures would be as enchanting as those in *Life*.

Still, they weren't all bad. His picture of McLean's Pond—water framed by branches, three barns sharp and clear against the sky—that picture was good. And his photograph of Jenny holding Indian paintbrush flowers in her hands, denim dress spread in a dark circle around her—it made him smile.

Heading home in the Studebaker, two new rolls of Kodak 616 film in his hands, Paul imagined scenes he would photograph.

"My next pictures will be better," he told his mother.

Taking her right hand from the wheel, she ran her fingers through his short-cropped hair.

"I'm sure they will be."

The final weeks of summer passed. With Jenny's help, Paul set up his aquarium in the west window of his bedroom. "Afternoon sunlight's good for plants and fish," she told him.

They filled the aquarium with water from a stream that fed the McLean pond. A day later they added plants and five silvery guppies.

"Four girls and a boy," Jenny said, pouring his fish into the aquarium. "Look at them! Nosing around the plants already. Healthy-looking critters."

A week before school began, Bill and Barbara Moran took them for a sail on the family's Lightning. Named *Art Spirit*, the boat was a gift Dr. Moran had presented to his wife a week after the Crystal One Gallery awarded her first place in their summer show. Her painting depicted a red Lightning heeling sharply starboard.

Then summer ended. To his surprise and distress, Paul learned—a day before school began—that he would have Miss Hart yet another year. It had to be a mistake, he thought. Seventh and eighth grade were always taught by Eva Christy, a teacher with blue hair who taught both grades in a combined class.

"This year's eighth grade was too big," Lena Howland explained. "So the school board decided yesterday to give seventh to Miss Hart."

That afternoon Paul sat on the front brick stoop, derailing his worries by composing imaginary pictures between his thumb and index finger.

No matter what school had in store, he would take photographs.

SEVEN

Rain

November 17, 1953

It was four o'clock, and except for claps of thunder, quiet prevailed in Rita Hart's seventh grade room. The day had been tough and, as dusk descended, she stood alone in her darkening room watching lightning play across the sky.

The nerve of those gossiping bitches, she thought.

Seven thirty in the morning and the two of them waltz into the teachers' room talking about her—unaware that she sat in the lavatory mere feet away.

"Never lifts a goddamned finger if it's not in the contract."

That was Marilyn Peterson.

"You said it!"

Becky Hall's scratchy voice.

"Ever see her after school when we're prepping kids for the Christmas play? Chaperone the Blue Water Girl Scouts? Attend a PTA meeting? Never! That gal left her get-up-and-go in Texas."

It was a bad start to the day, Rita mused, unable to forget the incident or what followed. Her brats picking the day to misbehave. Talking out of turn. Katherine Kimberly shooting spitballs. Black Owen James whispering to longhaired Brenda.

Then when they finally go home and it seems like it's over at last, that poison pen letter from Principal Eleanor Schlee shows up on the desk.

Now, picking it off her desk, she read it again.

"With the results of our first quarter assessment test in," it began, "it has come to my attention that four of the five nonfunctioning students at Crystal Elementary are in your seventh grade. The fact that they landed in your class is, of course, no fault of your own. But I am distressed that—after teaching them all of last year and for two months this fall—the test reveals zero progress. Our records show, Rita, that you have been employed here since 1927 and that you have done good work in the past. Yet I wonder, Miss Hart, if you've lost your commitment to the profession? Do make an effort to recapture the fiery spirit that served you well in earlier years."

Her heart raced. If they let her go early, she couldn't live on the rotten pension. And what then? Limp back to Texas carrying a carpetbag? Become a store clerk like the rat in Syosset who ran off with Charley? No. She'd show Eleanor Schlee her fiery spirit, all right—beginning with a fire she'd set beneath the goddamned Butterflies.

*   *   *

"We're going to try a new approach to reading," she told them the next morning, sitting on a piano bench pulled close to the Butterfly circle. "You're going to learn grammar, the structure of your English language. And in no time you'll be reading."

Across the circle, Gloria looked at her through vacant eyes. Brenda hid behind her hair. Black Owen fingered a closed book on his lap. Dumb Paul looked out the window.

What a hangdog bunch, she thought. So unlike her Robins and Bluebirds, the two groups already engaged in morning projects.

Rita Hart fought for composure. Stay positive, she told herself.

"When you know the parts of speech," she continued, "you will be astonished by how quickly you learn. Why, I wouldn't be surprised to find a reader or two among you by Christmas!"

She explained the purpose of verbs and nouns, adverbs and adjectives, prepositions, conjunctions, and pronouns.

"All right," she said, "we'll begin with Paul, who will do his best with chapter three. Start with the first sentence, Paul, the one about Captain Mack's boat."

Paul looked down at *I Can Read* open across his lap. He hunched his shoulders, feigning concentration. The only sound in the room was laughter from the Bluebirds. Owen James watched the wall clock as the minute hand swept by thirty seconds.

Paul was mute.

And Rita Hart was discouraged. She was lonely. Parents expected miracles she could not deliver. Her salary was abysmal. The years ran together because life never changed. And dummies. Always the goddamned dummies.

Discouragement that swept through every pore of Rita Hart's body turned to anger and a need to hurt.

"Let me show you how to do it," she hissed at Paul. "The sentence begins with the word *Boats*. It's a noun and subject of the sentence. The verb is *made*. *Wood*, *iron* and *aluminum* are nouns."

Going to the blackboard, she demonstrated how to diagram the sentence. She explained coordinating conjunctions, dependent and independent clauses, participial phrases, and correlative conjunctions.

She dropped the chalk and sighed.

"Your parents are college people," she said to Paul. "Your mother was valedictorian at New York University. How do I know these things? Because your mother and I talk, Paul. We used to think your eyes were the problem. They're not. Your problem is laziness. And it's going to end."

That afternoon, Paul found his mother waiting in the kitchen.

"Bring me *I Can Read*. Put that parts of speech list you brought home on the table."

He hung his coat in the closet and, while returning to the kitchen, heard the familiar *hiss* sound. In his mind he saw a stream of water-clear alcohol running onto ice.

"We'll start with the English grammar material using a sentence from your reader. That's Miss Hart's suggestion."

"'Captain Mack waits patiently while Joe baits the hook,'" Lena read.

It was nearly dark outside. Rain fell.

Fifteen minutes later, Lena snapped the book shut.

"Go."

One week later, Owen poked him in the ribs as they lined up for lunch.

"You see what she did with our homework this morning?"

Paul looked at him, uncomprehending.

"Threw it away!" he said. "Swept it off of her desk into the wastebasket without looking at it. Watch her tomorrow."

He did, and Owen was right.

For Rita Hart, the issue was coping. She could not endure the everyday confirmation of failure that came with correcting Butterfly work. She'd set a fire under them. And nothing changed.

Next day Paul walked Jenny home, then ran up the Laurel Path toward the Howland house. Excited by a plan that had come to him on the bus ride home, he dropped to his knees partway up the gravelly path. Using both hands, he scooped a hole in the sliding pebbles. In it he put *I Can Read* and some mimeographed papers.

Then he covered them with sand.

"You're late," Lena said. "No homework?"

"None. I was at Jenny's."

Before dark, Paul returned to the site of his buried homework, dragging behind him two cedar clapboards left by the workmen who'd built the Howland house. These he placed side to side over the pebble-concealed book. Protection, he thought, pleased by his ingenuity.

It worked, and he made a routine of the deception. He'd walk from the bus to Jenny's house every school day afternoon and—once she'd fed her fish and they'd split a peanut butter sandwich—he took the Laurel Path home. Into the pebbles went *I Can Read* and workbook papers. He retrieved them damp and sandy every morning. But he brushed off the sand and everything dried by the time the bus reached Crystal Elementary.

When school closed in late November for Thanksgiving vacation, Paul followed his familiar path through the laurel grove. The day was clear and unseasonably warm as he covered his book with stony earth.

"What are you doing?"

Startled, he looked up to see Jenny standing in the path.

How could he explain? He was mute until Jenny broke the silence.

"Okay. So you've buried your book and papers. You plan to leave them in dirt the next four days?"

"It's not dirt," he said, surprised by the anger in his voice.

He scooped up pebbles and dropped them *plip-plip-plip* so they danced on the green cover of his book. Above him, Jenny assumed her thinking pose, index finger of her left hand against her lower lip.

She didn't understand, he realized. So he told her why he hid the books and papers, that he could no longer stand homework sessions with his mother, who grew furious with him, and that hiding the stuff was a great solution because Miss Hart never checked Butterfly work.

"Still, you shouldn't do it," she said, kneeling down beside him in the laurel grove. "Leave your book at my house this vacation. It will be safe. Monday morning I'll give it to you at the bus stop.

"Better still," she added, "I can teach you the parts of speech. They're a cinch."

Tightness in his chest flared to anger. A cinch, he thought. And it was—for her. Everything in school was a cinch for Bluebirds and Robins. Their minds sucked in reading and math like summer grass drinking rain. It was different for Butterflies, each trapped in a glass cage unable to enter the easy world.

"You're dumb," he said, leaping to his feet. "You don't know anything."

Jenny backed away, tripping on a tangle of laurel roots and falling in her haste to escape. She righted herself quickly, and stood. Her face went pale. Then crimson.

In time her fists uncurled and the muscles of her jaw relaxed. She looked at him boldly.

"I spoke up," she began, "because what will happen if it rains on the stuff you buried? And I could teach you diagramming if you'd give me the chance."

She straightened, the memory of his words rekindling anger. "Suit yourself. Do what you want. Let your book rot in hell for all I care."

Jenny turned and departed. He watched her progress down the sloping path by movement of the green laurel. He didn't turn away until the leaves were still.

*   *   *

Thanksgiving dinner started with George Howland's reading from *The Book of Common Prayer*.

"'Keep us temperate in all things,'" he began, head bowed to the table. "'Keep us diligent in our callings.'"

Lena meanwhile sipped her cocktail, noting that George's bald spot had expanded.

Thank God for vermouth, she thought, drinking silently as her husband prayed.

Paul moped through dinner in a bad mood that lasted two more days. On Sunday he rallied enough to put film in the Box Brownie and set out for Fuller Farm, a place he'd never been before.

Climbing a wood rail fence at the east corner of Mary McLean's land, he dropped to a tangle of bittersweet. He plowed through its scratching tendrils until the vines gave way to a black-birch forest that seemed to go on forever. Then the trees thinned to reveal a hillside of brown November grass. On top of the hill six cows stood silhouetted against the fog-shrouded West Hills.

That wasn't all.

A quarter mile to Paul's left was a ramshackle barn and sag-roofed house. Next to the house, an exceptionally tall man in cowboy hat and boots stood watching him. Closer by, two men swung machete knives in a field of green cabbage.

"Hola, Gringo," the oldest said, the wrinkled lines of his weathered face drawn into a smile. "You have camera? Come to take our pictures?"

The younger man put his hand on the old man's shoulder. "My papa, Guillermo," he said. "He has seventy-nine years. Born in Puerto Rico. Before cars. Before airplanes. Take his picture."

Paul wanted to. But the tall stranger by the farm kitchen door made him uneasy.

"No worry," said the younger man. "That Eduardo Fuller. The boss. Eduardo crazy from war. Crazy at Guadalcanal."

The sky darkened over the West Hills.

"I'll photograph you together," Paul said.

He slid his camera's near-silent shutter to take the first picture. He advanced film and took two more, the workers' silver-bladed knives prominent in every frame.

Suddenly, clouds that had promised rain all afternoon delivered in torrents.

"Your camera!" said the old man, who pulled from his pocket a black oily rag. He wrapped it around the Kodak Brownie.

"Go! Go! Your camera okay now."

At the edge of the black-birch forest, Paul turned. A quarter mile distant, the two men plodded toward the Fuller barn through driving rain.

*　　*　　*

"You're soaked," Lena said. "Now just don't stand there. Look at the puddle you've made on my linoleum. Ye gods! I washed that floor this morning!"

Minutes later, Paul removed the bandage-like rag Guillermo had wrapped around the camera. To his amazement, the camera was dry.

In his room that night, Paul didn't pull the shade that blocked the flashing tower light. From his bed he watched its red pulsations magnified by raindrops running down the glass. None of it bothered him. The storm had a comforting sound, and he forgot there was school in the morning.

He awoke late, and remembering the buried book, charged down the Laurel Path. He stopped short at the burial place, pulling *I Can Read* from the pebbles and sodden earth. Green dye dripped from its cover. When he opened the book, its pages were gray mush.

Running for the bus, he held the book away from his body to avoid dripping dye.

"Told you so," Jenny said, her satisfaction changing to alarm when she saw the book's miserable condition.

"Throw it over the fence. Now. Tell her you lost it. It's better than..."

But the bus was already squeaking to a stop, its door folding open indifferently.

They got to school before Miss Hart. Paul, unsure what to do, looked past his desk to a floor-level shelf of textbooks and teacher supplies. There—just right of center—were two copies of *I Can Read*.

Glancing at the door, he took one of the two from its shelf and pushed his own mushy-wet text into the empty slot. The book's spine looked almost perfect except for a mud spot.

Rapidly now, for Miss Hart would arrive any moment, Paul wiped the book with his shirtsleeve. He was admiring his work when Miss Hart entered the room in a fluster. Months would pass before she found the ruined book. By then it wouldn't matter.

EIGHT

Eye

December 19, 1953

All day, Lena climbed up and down the attic stairs—retrieving candles, garlands, and everything else needed for her neighborhood Christmas party. At four o'clock, she checked her watch and shook her head in worry. In three rapidly vanishing hours, the first of two dozen guests would shake the antique carriage bell by the door—a signal that her annual party was under way. She called it "my neighborhood Shindig," reminding George that very morning that today's party was her "eighth annual," the event dating back to their first delightfully raucous postwar celebration in 1945.

Invitations to the 1953 event had been mailed just three days earlier—a delay Lena attributed to her husband's objection to several neighbors she wanted to invite. At issue were Sylvan Road people who'd been to past Shindigs, but behaved badly. Lena did agree to drop Joe and Edna Shadner. Their thriving rubbish collection business made them one of Sylvan Road's wealthiest residents. But when Joe was in his cups, as he'd been in 1950 and '51, he'd pinched Ina Chaffe twice on her rear end, and got into a fistfight last Christmas with Ina's husband. What to do about Dan and Janet Smith was a more difficult decision. The Smiths had a boundary dispute with their neighbor and used the annual Shindig to shout at their unfortunate abutter.

In the end, George mailed Dan and Janet's invitation.

"Okay. You win. The fracas is amusing. But I stand fast this Christmas on my motion to drop the Steins," George said, forgetting that he'd made the same proposal last year.

"We can't," Lena told him. "David's strange but harmless. And there's nothing wrong with Rachel. Besides, we've got to invite them. They're 'chosen people.'"

"Very funny. All right. They come."

On matters of entertainment, George—uncharacteristically—deferred to his wife.

At four thirty on D-Day afternoon, Millie Daniels "came breezing in," as Lena later described it, and was immediately put to work polishing silverware and carrying plates from the cupboard. Then it was time to take the ham from the oven. As Lena handed pot holders to Millie, she told the young woman how much she appreciated her help, thinking as she spoke of Millie's three boys under seven and not a husband to show for any of them.

Finally it was a quarter to seven with fifteen minutes to go before ringing bells would announce the start of Shindig 1953. At that moment, Millie reported to Lena that there wasn't room in the downstairs closet for the heavy coats the guests would surely wear on such a cold night. Lena told her to hover by the closet and send people upstairs—first door on the left to Paul's room—once the coat rack filled.

"Oh, how is he?" Millie asked, recalling the war years when she was in high school and babysitting Paul while Lena worked at Grumman. "I liked him. He was such a nice little boy. I pushed him in the blue carriage around the circle while he fluttered his hands at the trees—"

"He's doing fine," Lena said, cutting her short. "Paul will be in his room. But guests can leave coats on his bed."

Alone in the kitchen, Lena plucked a red-and-green cocktail glass from the waiting stack. She'd wanted a drink hours ago, but had put it off. Now she poured her cocktail, the glass pleasingly cool in her hand. Leaning back against the chrome counter, she admired the holiday plates and napkins and the ham Millie had rescued from the oven at the just-right moment. Then sleigh bells jingled at the door and Lena went to greet the first of her neighbors.

Meanwhile, Paul had set up his mother's card table in his bedroom. On its red Naugahyde top, he placed a new photograph album his father had given him the week before.

"Call it a Christmas present in advance," George had said, handing

Paul the white-paged book and three crinkly cellophane bags of black New Ace corners. "It's a better repository for pictures than the shoe box under your bed."

Now Paul opened the album to its first page. At his elbow, beneath the glow of a gooseneck lamp, he stacked photographs in the order in which he'd taken them, birthday pictures first, starting with a close-up of Jenny holding the aquarium. There was another of Jenny taken that same day in McLean's pasture, her denim dress spread circle-like around her on the grass. And there was Jenny and Mary on Mary's swing, a cat's cradle of intertwined string between their fingers. He slid New Ace corners onto the first picture and was picking up a second when a slant of light on the ceiling alerted him to the opening door.

"Excuse me. Excuse me. I don't mean to bother you but..."

He turned to see an old woman just entering, her hair set in parallel rows of gray curls. A tawny glass-eyed fox fur hung from one shoulder, its teeth clamped to its tail so the fur formed a circle looping up and around her neck.

"Is it real?" he asked.

"Everyone loves my fox!" she said, removing it in a graceful pirouette before dropping it on his bed. "Certainly it is real. Or was. Dead now, of course."

He recognized her as the woman who lived alone in a green ranch by the bus stop. Like the fox, her husband was dead.

In quick succession, two other guests draped coats on the bed. The second was their closest neighbor, Bob Lyford. "Selling these, are you?" he asked, nodding his head toward the photographs.

Paul told him he was not.

"Just as well," he replied, hooking his thumbs through red suspenders tight against a white shirt. "No money in photographs. On this island the wealth is in real estate. Bet on it, my boy."

Half an hour later, as Paul pressed a photo with licked New Ace corners onto the second album page, he became aware of a man standing behind to him. And he sensed, as he looked up, that the man had been there a while. The stranger had curly black hair—the curls straight up all over his head. Like Albert Einstein, Paul thought.

The man picked up a photograph of Mary's care-worn face. And Paul remembered how angry Jenny was that day when he pointed the camera in Mary's face.

"Nice," the man said. "I assume you took this?"

Before Paul could answer, the man grabbed another small picture and held it close to his face. "Holy shit!"

The Einstein man drew his index finger to his lips.

"Excuse my French. But where did this come from?"

It was the photograph of old Guillermo and his son, each with an arm wrapped about the other's shoulder.

Paul studied the stranger. He had a craggy face. Alert. Kind-looking.

Questions he asked were easy to answer. Paul told him how he'd discovered the harvesters last Thanksgiving, that he was twelve and in sixth grade. And no, he did not speak Spanish.

"My name's David Stein," the man said, shaking Paul's hand. "I'm a photographer. Like you."

David glanced at his watch, cocking his head to one side as if trying to decipher a word from muffled conversations downstairs.

"Your stuff is good," he said. "Keep shooting. Shoot a roll every week. No. Make that three."

Dropping his coat on the bed, David turned to leave. But midway through the doorway he stopped and came back.

"I studied at the Student Art League in New York City. That's where the best photographers learn their craft. What I mean to say is, it's a place where the best of the best go to school."

Then he stopped speaking, cocking his head slightly as he looked at Paul.

"You know what? Your work is as good—or better—than lots of student work I saw at the League. No, I'm not kidding. The big difference between you and those others is that they were at least eighteen years old. Most in their twenties. And you? Twelve!

"Paul," he said, "I take photographs for a newspaper called *The Mirror*. My photographs are like yours because your style of photography is my favorite. I mean portraits of people and scenics like your pond picture over there. I do a lot of other shooting for the paper: politicians, cops, car wrecks, murders. I could do without the murders and wrecks."

Paul asked if he took pictures for *Life*.

"No," he said, laughing. "That's a nut I haven't cracked. Why do you ask? You read *Life*?"

Looking away, Paul felt the familiar no-escape trap. Everything came back to the one question.

He looked at David. "I don't read *Life*. I don't know how to read. I look at the pictures."

David's eyes grew wide. He leaned forward, a smile breaking across his face.

"Hell's bells, kid," he said, "nobody reads *Life*! *Life* is about pictures. My God, the photographers they have. It's unbelievable. Those wonderful Ernst Haas pictures of New York. Phil Halsman's movie stars. Eugene Smith. Now holy living Jesus, *there's* a giant if there ever was one."

David paused.

"Where's your camera?" he asked. "Can you get it?"

Standing so fast that he sent the chair skidding along the floor, Paul opened his second bureau drawer where he kept the Box Brownie. He lifted the camera by its leather strap and put it on the table.

"Eastman and Kodak," David said, picking it up and turning it in his hands. "You've got an oldie here, all right. Any film in it?"

When Paul shook his head, David separated the camera into its halves. He put its black cardboard shell on the card table and squinted into the other half while tripping the camera's shutter.

"The camera that jump-started photography. This one's nineteen-twenty, I'd say. Maybe twenty-five."

Putting the two halves of the camera back together, David returned it to the table. As Paul reached for it, David squatted down in front of him, folding his arms on the table, chin propped on his hands.

"It's a good beginner's camera," he said. "I'm glad you have it. But you need a better lens."

He stood up. "Got to go back to the party."

Then he was gone, waving once to Paul from the landing.

*　　*　　*

Scanning the crowded living room, David spotted Rachel by the fireplace. When their eyes met he knew her thoughts by her expression.

Where had he been, anyway? Why had he left her alone in this crowded room standing by a mantel decorated with red-eyed snowmen, a Christmas tree blinking in the corner?

She was an attractive woman thirty-seven years old, with jet-black hair tied in a bun at her neck. Rachel was long accustomed to male eyes sweeping across her body when she looked up from her reference desk at

Crystal Public Library. Accustomed, yes. But still, David should not have left her alone in this goyim place full of drunks. Hard enough dealing with Sylvan Road people one at a time, let alone a pack of them.

Now she made her way toward David, sidestepping chatting couples, her annoyance ebbing because she was infinitely happy to catch sight of her husband even though he'd left her too long.

David smiled as Rachel came close. And he told her about a twelve-year-old in the house who took amazing landscape photos and portraits of his girlfriend and Puerto Rican workers he'd somehow met at a farm near the West Hills. Her face softened as she listened. It was David's love of photography and his enthusiasm for life that had so attracted her when she married him at nineteen, and he only a sophomore then at the Art League.

So show him your darkroom," she said. "Take him on the Long Island Railroad to New York. Go to *The Mirror*. Let him see how photographers work."

And he clapped his hands in delight because neither possibility had occurred to him, and he wanted to do both immediately. That is, if the boy's parents would allow it. When he stopped speaking for a moment, Rachel pointed to her watch and whispered to him that she needed to leave soon because she'd had it with the Christmas tree and cigarette smoke thick enough to cut with a knife. He put his hand on her shoulder and, leaning close, told her he wanted to leave early, too, and they would, except he had one thing to do.

And for fifteen minutes, David waited to speak with George Howland, who stood in front of his green couch cornered by talkative Wally Freeman. Shifting his feet, David waited until Wally staggered off to the kitchen where tired Millie served drinks.

"Have you seen your son's photographs?" David said, stepping close to George.

Backing away, George hit the couch with both feet. Silently he fell back onto its cushions, striving as he did to balance a half-filled tumbler of martini. A second later he bounced to his feet, drink still in hand.

"Your son," David shouted over the party noise. "He has the eye."

NINE

Lens

"It's the longest cold wave in twenty years."

The sky was winter blue. Wind lashed the oaks. Lena, still in her nightgown, vigorously swept the kitchen floor.

"Dorothy and Dick talked about it on their program. It's fourteen degrees in New York City. That's the same temperature as Caribou, Maine."

Indeed, the arctic chill that had swept across Long Island Sound on Christmas Day had hit Crystal with sufficient force to shear branches off maples and birches. A foot of snow clung to the ground.

"Best sledding yet," Jenny said as she set out with Paul for Dead Man's Hill in midafternoon.

No one knew how Dead Man's had acquired its name, though children younger than seven—too small to risk a Flexible Flyer ride between rocks and trees—thought they knew. To them, it was the steep gully where older kids went and sometimes failed to return.

Those who dared to sled on Dead Man's Hill did nothing to correct the perception. For sledding Dead Man's gave license to swagger. Besides, everyone knew the story of Sally Ann Henson. She had flown sideways off the boulder jump halfway down, then plunged headfirst into juniper bushes. Her mother rushed her to Crystal General where, according to the story, a nurse pulled juniper needles out of Sally's eyes. Still they talked about Sally, even though her accident happened in 1950.

But on that cold January third morning, as Paul and Jenny headed for Dead Man's—pulled sleds bouncing behind on ice-rutted Sylvan Road—Sally Ann was not in their thoughts. Jenny's sled was her big Christmas gift: a Paris Flyer with scarlet runners that matched her new parka.

"You look like Red Riding Hood," Paul said.

She feigned a teeth-bared lunge for his throat. He stepped back, laughing.

"I said Red Riding Hood. Not the wolf."

Ice covered the snowpack on Dead Man's Hill. Paul went first, his sled accelerating instantly to a frightening speed. But he leaned right to avoid Danger Oak, as they called it. The boulder jump sent him flying so far that he thought he'd end up in juniper. But he landed dead center on track and rode the sled until it stopped on the flats.

"Watch out, Jenny!" he shouted. "It's like glass."

Already Jenny was speeding through the first steep drop—a streak of red parka and scarf. She went airborne on the boulder jump longer than anyone ever soared. The juniper patch was far behind, but slamming the fallen locust tree at the bottom of the hill seemed inevitable. Jenny rolled off the Paris Flyer a second before her sled hit the tree, rose five feet in the air, and landed upside down on top of a laurel bush.

"Yikes!" Jenny said, jumping to her feet. "My poor sled!"

But it was all right except for a chip of paint missing from a runner.

"We can't sled here today. It's a death trap," she added, and Paul readily agreed.

So they walked to Jenny's house, sleds rattling behind.

"I'm getting my Rhode Island Reds in April," she told him. "Day-old chicks. Dad will convert that barn on our property to a proper chicken house. He'll build a wire run, too, so my Reds can be safe from foxes."

They split a peanut butter and jelly sandwich at Jenny's. Then, sitting together on the thick carpet in Jenny's room, she read aloud from *Marsha*, a book about a seventeen-year-old girl and her boyfriend, Steve Holliday. Later they made chocolate chip cookies while, in an adjacent room, Bill Moran practiced a Bach partita on his cello.

When Paul looked to the kitchen window, it was black night.

Leaving Jenny's driveway, he looked skyward through bare branches. Above was the white highway of north-trending stars that he recognized as the Milky Way. The galaxy, and the three stars of Orion's belt, comprised what he knew of astronomy.

When shivering interrupted sky watching, he fast-walked to his driveway.

Nearing the house, Paul was surprised to see somebody alone on the front steps, the slightly stooped figure illuminated in a circle of light. When the door opened and he heard his parents' voices, he left his sled in the driveway and followed a single set of prints past his dad's rose briar onto the snowy lawn. Ahead on the shoveled stoop was David Stein, a brown shopping bag in his hand. George Howland held the front door open and, leaning out, spotted Paul.

"Well, there he is now!" George exclaimed. "Let's all of us come in before we catch pneumonia."

David and Paul stepped into the entryway hall. George cracked his knuckles. Lena asked David if he wanted a drink.

"Nothing like a fireplace," David said, ignoring Lena's question as he nodded toward oak and maple logs crackling in the screen-covered fireplace.

"You can say that again," George said, pleased to have a conversation going. "Let's sit by the fire. Lena will bring us drinks."

David smiled but shook his head.

"No. It's a weekday night. Got to be at work early tomorrow. Another time, thank you. I stopped by because I have something for Paul. Call it a late holiday gift. It's something—"

"You didn't have to do that," Lena interjected, pointing to piles of toys beneath the lighted Christmas tree. "Check out his loot. Chess set from Great-Uncle Harry, a forty-piece Erector set including a motor and lights—and that ping-pong ball gun. I could kill my sister for giving it to Paul. We have ping-pong balls bouncing all over the house for God's sake. George stepped on one yesterday. I thought he'd go flying."

She stopped and looked at David, who sensed her disapproval of his bringing a gift. Had he broken some unwritten goyim rule? Clearly she didn't like him. And why, he wondered. Was it his religion or the clothes he wore? Would it be different if he had a crew cut?

David was glad when George broke an uncomfortable silence.

"Well, David, I don't want to waste your time. You're a busy man, and you've brought a present for Paul. So why don't the two of you go to the TV room so you can show him what's in the box."

Though they called it a TV room, the twelve-inch-screen Magnavox that lent its name to the space was seldom used. Its blank green face, staring forgotten in a corner, was dwarfed by a large captain's desk. It had originally been owned by Ebenezer Howland, Boo Speedball's eccentric father, who had risen to captain rank in the Union Army.

"Nice desk," David said, placing a robin's-egg-blue box at its center. He sat momentarily in the desk's swivel chair, then leapt to his feet.

"Whoops. Almost forgot this," he said, reaching into his back pocket to remove a second present the size of a cigarette pack.

Dropping into the swivel chair a second time, David turned to face Paul.

"Might as well open 'em," he said

Neither was gift-wrapped. Paul slid a rubber band off the smaller package and lifted its top. Inside was an instrument. It had a round silver dial on one side, the dial covered with numbers. A red needle moved slightly as Paul studied the contraption under the gooseneck lamp. And he worried because it looked too complicated to understand. Like the Erector set beneath the tree, it was a thing he'd never use.

"Open the blue box," David urged, leaning forward in the chair. "The big one."

When he held back, still worried about the small device, David reached over Paul's head, flipped the cover off the blue box, and plucked from it a leather case that undoubtedly held a camera.

With tenderness and some befuddlement—for he had no experience with children—David handed it to Paul.

It was heavier than the boy expected and, when he removed its leather case, the camera shone with the metallic radiance of an airplane wing. Wheels and dials covered its surface. But it was the lens that fascinated Paul. Recessed within a silver column, its rounded glass looked like a black reflective pool.

"It's an Argus," David said. "Made in America and well made, if I do say so myself. F-stop of two-point-eight down to f-22. Shutter speed fast enough to stop an acrobat in midair."

Paul was hardly aware of David's voice. Instead he dreamt of summer and how he'd hold the camera's window-like finder to his eye and photograph eelgrass that grew by the water's edge at Clam Shell Beach, and he saw in his mind's eye the sparkle of blue salt water beyond the grass. And he imagined photographing Jenny in her black bathing suit, the picture returned from Eastman Kodak magnificently clear.

Did the Argus really belong to him—this camera a *Life* photographer might proudly use?

"Of course, there's a bit more to picture-taking with the Argus than the old Box Brownie," David said, reaching for the camera. He leaned back in Ebenezer Howland's old swivel chair and, with a sweep of his hand, motioned to a smaller chair by the desk.

Paul watched and listened.

"Those numbers on the lens rim—they're the f-stops I told you about. They regulate how much light comes through the lens. There's an inverse ratio between the f-stops and shutter speeds you see here on the round dial. So if you're shooting at f-11 at one-fiftieth of a second and you decide to increase shutter speed to one one-hundredth of a second, then you gotta stop down to f-8 to keep a consistent exposure."

David looked at Paul—too quickly to notice the boy's change of expression. For Paul no longer looked at the camera or listened. Slumped forward, he stared at a twisted paper clip and a chewed pencil stub on Ebenezer's desk. Excitement he'd felt minutes before was gone. Had the light been stronger in the room, or David less involved with the Argus, the photographer would have noticed the pallor of the boy's face, and how the iris and pupil of his astigmatic eye had drifted off center.

For Paul knew that, despite the happiness he'd enjoyed with the Kodak Box Brownie, he'd hit a glass wall in photography. Just as he did in every endeavor. He'd never learn to use a good camera. His dream of becoming a photographer—a dream David had encouraged and he'd thought possible—was out of reach.

"Now the other thing we need to go over," David continued, "is how to use this Weston meter. It's a gem. Accurate as all get-out."

Pushing away the Argus, David held the light meter beneath the gooseneck lamp. As Paul watched, a red needle moved within the meter's glass window. It wavered before stopping on number forty.

"That's your guide number," David said, excitement in his voice. "See those other numbers below the needle? They match guide numbers."

He leaned back in the swivel chair and smiled. "Why, with a Weston meter, you can…"

And he noticed for the first time Paul's expression, noticed that Paul appeared sad and lost. And the photographer was angry with himself for failing to see the effect he'd had on the child. My God, he thought. Here I've carried on like a college professor and the kid's twelve. A kid who can't read for some reason and likely struggles in school. Holy shit. For the love of Mike. Here's a boy who took wonderful pictures with the box camera, and me arrogant enough to think I could improve his creativity. And who are you, David Stein, to make that assumption? Childless. Forty-seven-years-old. A man who needs a camera in his hands to feel at ease. Who am I to presume?

He put his hand on Paul's shoulder.

The room was quiet but for the tick of a wind-up clock on top of the TV.

"Listen," David said, "forget everything I told you about the new stuff."

Taking his hand from Paul's shoulder, he lifted the light meter from the desk. "Put this in a bureau drawer. You don't need it. It's a tool, see? Some photographers use light meters. Some don't. Understand?"

Paul nodded.

"Got some paper?" the photographer asked. "Tape? A pencil?"

A drawer in Ebenezer's desk contained paper and tape. Paul handed David the chewed pencil.

Folding the paper, the photographer sketched a circle in the upper left corner. From its circumference he sketched radiating lines. "The sun," he said. "I'm not the world's best artist."

To the right of the sun he wrote f-11.

Below it he drew blotchy shapes in a little box. Some he shaded with pencil.

"Clouds."

Next to the clouds he put f-8.

"That's your setting for cloudy days."

Using cellophane tape, David fastened his sketches to the camera's leather case. He handed camera and case to the boy.

"Okay," he said, stretching out the word as he studied Paul's face for comprehension. "That's all it takes to use the Argus."

David set the shutter speed wheel at one-hundredth of a second and told Paul to leave it there.

"So when you take a picture in shade, set your lens at f-8. If you're in the sun, use f-11. Can't remember? Check my funny drawings."

David removed the camera's bottom plate and showed Paul how to load film. They practiced focusing.

"You've got thirty-six exposures here," David said, "three times as many as the old Box Brownie."

He paused. "I'll develop your film," he said. "And teach you to use a darkroom—if that's something you want to learn."

*   *   *

At the front door, David said good-bye to George and Lena. They stepped aside as the photographer—hatless and coatless but for a worn cotton jacket—stepped into the winter night.

TEN

Contest

February 7, 1954

A month passed happily for Paul. He took three rolls of film with the Argus, and David developed them all.

"You're improving," he told the boy. "Each roll's better than the one before. Especially that last one with the picture of Mary McLean. It's a corker."

Paul had taken the *exposure*—a term he'd just begun to use—in Mary's barnyard on a blustery Saturday morning. He'd gone to the farm alone.

That surprised Mary.

"Where, pray tell, is Pigtails?" she asked, meeting him at the pantry door.

"Probably asleep," Paul said, and offered to bring in firewood.

She didn't protest, and held his camera while he did the chore.

"Spiffy little thing," she said of the camera, when he returned with an armful of logs. Then they drank cocoa in her kitchen.

Mary asked what Jenny was up to.

"She's the smartest in our class by a long shot," he told her.

"No surprise there. The girl's a caution." She laughed. "Gave you a talking-to last summer. Remember? You took my picture with the black camera out in the barnyard. Jenny called you *impolite*, and didn't your ears turn red!"

Embarrassed, he looked into his mug. Mary leaned close. Her bony hand clutched his arm.

"You can take my picture anytime."

"Really?"

"Look at you," she said. "Happy as a clam in summer."

When it was time for him to leave, Mary twisted a black shawl over her shoulders and followed him to the entryway. There she paused, gnarled hand resting on the latch, eyes adjusting to the snowy glare.

Paul made three quick photographs, each at a different lens setting. *Apertures*, the settings were called. Take the same picture at different apertures and you are *bracketing*. Bracketing increases the chance of a just-right picture.

He'd learned a lot from David.

Paul shook Mary's hand good-bye.

"Give my love to Pigtails," she said.

*　　*　　*

As he discovered the next morning, Pigtails was about to embark on an adventure.

That information came from Miss Hart, who swished into seventh grade on February seventh in an orange taffeta dress. Smiling at them, she put her fingertips together one to one, creating a steeple she touched to her chin.

"Last night I had a call from our Crystal Elementary principal, Mrs. Eleanor Schlee. As luck would have it, the North Shore League of Exceptional Schools has invited our school to participate in its annual Top of the Island Spelling Bee. And here's the biggest surprise of all: our Jenny Moran will represent Crystal Elementary, as will Hanna Abelson, an eighth grader some of you may know."

Jenny sat straight in her chair, eyes wide with surprise.

"I must explain," Miss Hart said, raising her hand to keep their attention, "why Jenny's selection is unusual. Of ten students picked from North Shore League Schools, only one is in seventh grade. That's Jenny. She earned her place through an exceptional performance on three qualifying tests—taken, I might add, while the rest of you were at recess."

The class then spent twenty minutes wrangling over team names proposed for the Abelson-Moran duo. *Warriors* was already taken by

Glen Cove Country Day, the name honoring a long-dispatched Indian tribe that had once roamed the cove. Bayville Elementary picked *Pine Islanders*. Kids at Mutton Town Village School chose *Word Butters*.

When Brenda Long timidly proposed *Crystal Chandeliers*, laughter met the suggestion. Miss Hart rejected *Blue Water Rompers* as "silly." But Katherine Kimberly's follow-up proposal—*Blue Harbor Renegades*—passed with a near-unanimous vote.

"Renegades it is," Miss Hart said, banging her desk with a plastic ruler.

With the five-school contest three weeks away, Jenny used every available hour to prepare. Afternoon recess was her practice time with Hanna. The sessions took place in Eva Christy's eighth-grade room.

"Wait until we have Mrs. Christy next September!" Jenny told Paul. "You'll love her."

Twice during February, Paul took the Laurel Path to Jenny's. Both times she was practicing words with her mother and he stayed to listen.

"*Catamaran*," Barbara Moran said, reading from a notebook. When Jenny spelled all nine letters without pausing for breath, her mother signaled thumbs-up. Jenny got *surefire* right, and *fracas* too.

Bill Moran, practicing his cello in the living room, quit midway through his Bach piece

"Okay, smarty-pants," he said, "let's hear it for *chlorophyll* and *eczema*!"

When she missed *eczema*—substituting an *x* for *c*—Bill's cello groaned a base chord.

"Jeepers, Dad," Jenny yelled. "I'm not Einstein!"

Barbara Moran laughed. "Don't listen to the guy. You're going to ace the bee. Guaranteed."

On the morning of the contest, Jenny left for Hofstra College at eight thirty, the only passenger in Miss Hart's maroon Ford. Hanna Abelson, a shy girl with brown hair trimmed to a Dutch cut, came to the college with Eva Christy.

Half an hour later, all four teams sat on stage near Chief Judge Andrew Joyce. Before them, two hundred parents and teachers filled the auditorium.

"Welcome to Hofstra and our Fourteenth Annual Top of the Island Spelling Bee," he said, then turned to address the contestants.

"In decisions relating to this bee, we three are your gods. The dark-haired lady on my left is Circe. Athena is to my right. Call me Zeus."

He paused for laughter and, when there was none, reintroduced himself as an assistant English professor. Circe was an eighth-grade teacher in Baldwin and Athena proofread books for a publishing house in Queens.

Pine Islanders were first to go, knocked out by misspelling *annulment* and *vignette*. Warriors of Glen Cove Country Day fell to *psychiatry* and *transept*. Word Butters of Mutton Town Village School were eliminated by default when Athena detected whispering at their table. *Narcolepsy* knocked out Renegade Hanna Abelson.

Thirty minutes into the contest, the two survivors faced off: Jenny Moran from the Renegades, and Gold Coaster Cameron Davis, a handsome flaxen-haired eighth grader from Center Island School.

For three rounds, the lone contestants held their own with words that included *deductible, lesion,* and *defendant.* When Cameron Davis missed *anathematize,* the auditorium went silent. For the anticipated championship word was next—and if Jenny got it right, newcomer Crystal Elementary would have the title.

On stage by the podium, Athena whispered to Zeus. Briefly, they appeared to disagree. Then Zeus smiled.

"Young lady," he said, your potential championship word is *antidisestablishmentarianism.*

On a square of paper held in one palm, Jenny wrote quickly—looked at her word—and crossed it out.

"May I have the Webster pronunciation?"

Athena complied.

Then, with calm assurance, Jenny nailed the twenty-seven-letter word.

Pandemonium swirled through the auditorium as Judge Andrew Joyce declared Jenny Moran winner of the 1953 Top of the Island Spelling Bee.

"An unexpected coup for the Renegades," said Zeus, shouting to be heard over the din. "Remarkable too because Jenny Moran is the first-ever seventh grader to compete in this contest."

Minutes later, Paul and his classmates heard the news when Principal Schlee banged open their classroom door to bring good tidings, her entrance startling a likable though struggling substitute teacher.

Two days later, as the school's end-of-recess bell clanged, Paul caught up with Jenny as they neared the school entrance.

"Where did you learn to do that?" he asked. "I mean, spell the longest word in the world?"

"Oh, my gosh, you're only the ten thousandth person to ask me—and it isn't the world's longest word. It's longest in the English language. Maybe."

"So how come you know it?

"Phonics," she said. "And this."

From her blue jeans she pulled the amethyst stone that glistened smoky purple in the February sun.

"You had it with you?

"In the pocket of my blue dress. And I touched it, too. Then I spelled the word."

❋   ❋   ❋

On a Saturday morning not long after, Paul siphoned water from Jenny's aquarium while she rearranged aquatic plants. "Thank you," she said. "Water changes are hard to do alone."

They looked up when the front door opened and Barbara Moran, sorting letters and magazines, walked into the kitchen.

"Letter for you, Jenny. Postmark Oyster Bay."

"Spelling bee stuff probably. I'm busy, Mom. Would you read it to me, please?"

"Sure. This is interesting. Oversized card. The sender used an extra stamp."

Then there was quiet.

"'Cameron Davis here,'" Barbara began. "'You may wonder as you read this missive, why is Cameron writing me? No, I am not angry because you won the Bee. Quite the contrary. You're the smartest girl I ever met. And I will never forget…'"

Barbara stopped.

"Jenny?" she asked. "You want me to go on?

"You've started already, Mom. Yeah. Go ahead."

"'And I will never forget seeing you there at Hofstra, index finger raised to your red lips, left hand in your dress pocket as if spelling the longest word in the English language was an everyday thing to you.

"'What I am wondering is, would you come with me to *Creature from the Black Lagoon*? It starts Monday in Oyster Bay. My mother can drive us. If you'd rather see a different movie, we can. *A Star is Born* is playing in Crystal! My mom can bring us to either. Please call or write to me.

"'Your friend, Cameron

"'P.S. You've got great braids.'"

The fish aquarium siphon slipped from Paul's hands, spreading a white puddle on the Morans' green rug.

"Don't worry," Barbara said, her voice sympathetic as she threw a kitchen towel over the mess.

"Oh, my gosh, Mom," Jenny said, "What do I do now? You think I should go?"

"That's up to you. One thing is for certain. I will speak with Cameron's mother before any decisions are made."

Silently, Paul and Jenny finished up with the fish. Together they walked to the porch.

"Will you go?" he asked.

"No," she said. "I hardly remember him. I was thinking about words that day, not boys. I'm going to write to Cameron. I'll tell him my father won't let me. 'Course I'll talk to Dad first. Get him on board, so to speak."

She paused.

"Paul! Know what? Remember the chicken pen I told you about, the one my dad partitioned off in the barn? It's done! We pick up the chicks at Katy's Hatchery next month. My Rhode Island Reds at last!"

ELEVEN

Chicks

March 16, 1954

Winter reluctantly left the Island. The last patch of snow in Paul's yard finally melted. Ice vanished from McLean's Pond. Sounds of spring peepers filled the nighttime woods and, by the second week in March, Canada mayflowers bloomed on the forest floor.

One afternoon, a half hour after getting home from school, Paul picked up the ringing phone in the hallway.

It was Jenny.

"They're here!" she yelled into the receiver. "My chicks! All twelve of them! Katy's Hatchery called my dad at work this morning and told him they'd hatched. He drove to the hatchery, where they had the chicks in a cardboard box with holes in the sides and top for air. Dad left the box on my bed. When I carried it to the chicken house, these tiny little guys pecked my fingers through the holes. And they're only a few hours old.

"Come over. I'll be in the barn. Shut the door tight after you because they don't like drafts."

Grabbing his camera, Paul jumped from the porch, pressing the Argus to his side so it wouldn't jolt when he hit ground. Then he ran zig-zag down the path to Jenny's.

When he swung open the squeaky barn door—careful to pull it fast shut behind him—it took seconds for his eyes to adjust to the barn's mostly dark interior. Then he saw Jenny hunkered down next to her wooden brooder, a partially covered wooden box fitted with a lightbulb to warm the yellow-red chicks. Jenny watched her brood as she rocked back on her heels, arms clasped around her knees. Sunlight streaming through a dusty barn window illuminated her face.

"Jenny," he whispered, "would you pick up one Rhode Island Red and stay in sunlight?"

She lifted a chick from the fluffy mass and, in the waning afternoon light, held it to her chest. There in the viewfinder was the Jenny he loved—a girl who was kind and possessed a special grace. And the image he intended to make would hint at the wonderful essence of Jenny Moran. He reached for the shutter—and froze.

He'd overlooked the obvious. It was too dark in the barn for anything but a long exposure. A photographer needs a tripod for such an exposure. He had none.

If he took the picture holding the Argus in his hands, camera shake would ruin it.

Slowly, he lowered the camera. Yet in that very instant, even as he sighed in defeat, he noticed a solid oak timber—an ancient floor-to-ceiling barn support—mere inches away. And he leaned into it, head and shoulder jammed against the support as he touched the shutter release to make a quarter-second exposure through the wide-open Argus lens.

But the light was fading even as he hit the shutter. He made a second exposure at a half second, and a third at one second. And the sun disappeared behind clouds.

"You can sit down now," he told her.

"You a nut cake," she said, laughing. "Thank you for giving me permission to sit. Arf! Arf! Can I breathe too?"

She knelt by the brooder, then opened her hand and released the hours-old Rhode Island Red. It ran to the yellow clump of chicks beneath the brooder light.

Then she got up and flicked a switch on the barn wall. A single white bulb cast a circle of light that revealed a stack of magazines on the barn floor. A photograph of an alert white hen appeared on the topmost issue.

"*People's Poultry*," Jenny said, seeing Paul's interest. "My dad's nurse keeps Barred Plymouth Rocks. She subscribes to the magazine. When she learned I was getting chicks, she gave me her back issues. The thing I like best in *People's Poultry* is a column called 'Poultryman's Diary.' It's a real diary written by a poultry farmer named Jeb."

Picking the top magazine from the pile, Jenny sat cross-legged beneath the one electric light.

"Listen: 'I told Ma I'd check the hens one more time before turning in…'"

She stopped and looked at Paul. "I forgot to tell you one thing about 'Poultryman's Diary.' Ma isn't Jeb's mother. She's his wife. It took a while to figure that out."

He looked at her cross-legged on the barn floor, magazine folded back in her hands. Her brown hair glistened even in the electric light. He sat down next to her, legs Indian fashion like hers.

Jenny started reading again.

"'Ma told me to hurry on back after checking the hens because she had a pie in the oven. She made it from that last picking of apples on our Haralson tree, and promised me pie and ice cream before bed. But I was in for a bad surprise that night when I pushed open the shed door and saw snow swirling under the barn light just like the middle of winter, and here it is ten days before Thanksgiving. It was sticking to the ground, too, and I commenced to worry about the weight of wet snow on the poultry house roof. Then I pushed open the chicken house door and got my second bad surprise. The automatic water fount had clogged up again in the Leghorn pen, so I had a flood on my hands. And there were my foolish hens standing smack-dab in the middle of the flood. Thinking they were ducks, I guess. So I shut off the water and cleaned out the fount. Then I shoveled six wheelbarrow loads of wet litter, trundling each one out of the chicken house to dump in the snow. Afterwards there was fresh litter to carry in and spread. Last of all, I collected eggs and wound the alarm clock timer to snap on the lights at 4 a.m.

"'Outside the snow flew harder than ever. I had to shovel through a drift to get back into the house. And wasn't Ma mad at me for being gone so long and her pie getting cold. But she calmed down some when I told her about the snow and the flood and what-all else. Ma wants to sell the farm. It's too much for me, she says. Too much for one man to be out here in the Ohio Hills at seventy years of age with two thousand Leghorns.

"But we ate the pie, and don't them Haralson apples taste good with the ice cream. It put Ma in a better mood, and after a while she agreed that things are going pretty good. That new Rock Island Leghorn cross puts out a lot of eggs, and the white egg price is improving. In spite of problems, there's nothing quite like a poultry man's life here in Ohio. I guess that wraps it up for December. Sincerely, Jeb Edgecomb for *People's Poultry.*'"

* * *

Headlights glinted in the barn's east window. Then the door squeaked open and Barbara walked to the brooder where Paul and Jenny sat watching the chicks move about under the light.

"My goodness," she said. "It's late. You better trot home, Paul, or your parents will think we've kidnapped you. Want a flashlight?"

He thanked her but declined, for he knew every root and branch of the Laurel Path. Yet he worried as he walked, knowing he had missed supper.

But when he walked in and announced he was home, his father greeted him in a friendly way from the living room. His mother, grasping a chair back for balance, lifted a pot of mushroom soup from the stove.

"Lukewarm," she said.

In bed not long after, Paul's mind drifted for several moments in a transition zone between wakefulness and sleep—a place where ghosts of the just-lived day pass in fleeting images. Again he saw the reddish-yellow chicks and Jenny reading beneath the barn light. Mayflowers. A star-filled sky over the Laurel Path.

* * *

A misty rain fell Sunday morning. At eight thirty, David called.

"Well, my friend, it's a darkroom kind of day. I'm going down now to develop a Tri-X roll I shot yesterday when Rachel and I were out to Sunken Meadow. Have you got film for me?"

When Paul replied that he had exposed an entire roll and put another in the camera, he sensed David's pleasure.

Ten minutes later, he walked into the Steins' house. Rachel ushered him into the living room while David finished up in the cellar.

"He's hypnotized by his darkroom," she said. "Nothing to do but have patience. He'll clomp upstairs by and by."

Paul liked Rachel's easy manner, and her house where geraniums and ivy grew on windowsills.

Strange paintings on two walls fascinated him. In one framed piece, a fat hand on a blue background pointed a finger skyward. Another showed a figure of some sort—human or fish, he wasn't sure—floating in a box above an apple or a doorknob.

"They're by Matisse," Rachel said, noting his curiosity. "Henri Matisse. They're prints, of course—copies of originals. That one with the floating creature? It's a paper cutout Matisse named *Swimmer in the Aquarium.* The other one—that hand over there—it's another Matisse. But I know the painting you're looking at. Trying hard *not* to look, I should say. But you can't fool me."

It was a nude woman on a rumpled bed, her profile face looking toward the artist.

"Ingres," Rachel said. "*Obalisque.* Now, I could be jealous of that one. It's David's favorite. And wouldn't you think a photographer would have photographs in his house? Wouldn't you think that? Not David. He has *Obalisque.*"

She laughed. "I'm not jealous. He likes me best."

Footsteps sounded on the cellar stairs. And they turned to see David stoop to pass through the undersized cellarway door.

"My friend!" he said, seeing Paul. "The two of you quiet as conspiratorial mice while I'm down in the fumes.

"So Paul. Let's see what you've shot."

The small size of David's darkroom amazed Paul. No bigger than Lena's broom closet, it smelled like the science room at Crystal Elementary. An orange lightbulb at the center of the black-painted room cast pumpkin-colored light onto a table where implements lay in neat order: wooden tongs, stained trays, a glistening metal tank shaped like a small cake.

Standing in the middle of his kingdom, chest to feet covered by a plastic apron, David seemed to Paul like a great friendly bear standing proud in his cave, surrounded by things of tremendous importance.

When David asked Paul for his film, the boy pulled a yellow container from his pocket.

David opened it, spilling out the film canister.

"I see you've remembered your lesson from last week," he said. "You left the film end—we call it the leader—outside the canister. That makes loading the development tank easier.

"Lights out," he said, clicking an extension cord that shut off the pumpkin bulb.

"Soon you'll be loading this development tank by your lonesome. But no need to rush."

When a wall switch clicked to Paul's left, white light flooded the room.

Lifting an amber-colored jug, David poured liquid through a light-tight opening at the top of the tank. "Microdol-X," he said.

For twenty minutes, Paul watched David pour chemicals in and out of the development tank. Sometimes he flipped it over in his hands. Other times he left it untouched on the table. Absorbed in his work, he muttered names of chemicals.

"Pretty much done now," he said, pouring the last patch of chemistry from tank to bottle. "Nothing to do now but wash the film and see what you've been up to with the Argus."

After what seemed to Paul like an eternity, David turned off a faucet that, for the better part of a half hour, had poured tepid water onto the open development tank.

From the tank David pulled a black ribbon of glistening film. Pushing tortoiseshell glasses down over his eyes, he held the dripping film in front of the bare electric bulb.

"Okay," he said, peering at the film. "I see a house here. Exposure right, the house framed by a windowpane. Not bad, Paul. Then some more shots of...a driveway, it looks like. And the McLean field after a blizzard. Guess you took that one back in January."

David lowered the film, glancing down at Paul, who crowded close to see his negatives. "Cloud images through trees," he said. "Putting that new yellow filter to use, I see."

Holding the still-wet film in front of the bulb, David reached the final three images.

"Jesus," he muttered. "Jesus H. Christ. Now *there* is a picture. *There* is a photograph, my friend. Your cute girlfriend, I see. Holding what? A duck?"

"A chick."

Paul pressed close to see.

"It's a Rhode Island Red, Mr. Stein."

"Please. Name's David."

He moved the film to better align it with the light.

"Jesus, Paul. It looks like a studio portrait, what with the black background and all. How the hell did you do it?"

"I took the first at a quarter-second using a barn beam to steady the Argus. The second exposure is a half-second. The third a full second."

David hung the still-dripping film next to his roll of Tri-X.

"I'd like your permission to borrow your negs for a day or so," he said. "I want to bring them to the city. Our darkroom at the *Mirror* has Leitz enlargers. They have great optics. Best of the best. That's what this negative of your girlfriend deserves."

Paul happily gave his permission, and on a clear spring evening three days later, David bounded up the Howlands' flagstone steps, a manila envelope in his hand.

Paul opened the front door.

"This will put a smile on your face," David said. "Your photo made the rounds of our newsroom—where, I might add, it inspired a lot of smiles."

In the TV room, the photographer turned on the overhead light before pushing the envelope into the boy's hands.

"Open it!"

Lifting the hasp, Paul slid the photograph onto Ebenezer's desk. And stared. He'd taken a dozen pictures of Jenny since July. They were shadows compared to this. For here was Jenny's face looming out of darkness, her eyes revealing her love for a tiny creature. His photograph, he knew, was more than an image. It was a clue to the spirit of his friend.

"She's beautiful," he said.

"Damn straight, she's beautiful!" David replied, his voice practically booming. "And there's something else you need to know. While your print was washing in the darkroom, our layout editor, Joe Emerson, walks in and picks it out of the tray.

"Nice shot, Davie,' he says, 'we'll use it on the jump page Friday.' So I tell Joe it's not my photo, that the picture was made by a twelve-year-old in Crystal. So Joe looks at me like I'm pulling his chain. Then he knows it's the truth.

"'That's one talented kid,' he says, big grin on his face. 'Tell him we'll buy his photo.'"

Reaching into the pocket of his khaki pants, David retrieved a crinkled ten-dollar bill.

"It runs tomorrow," he said. "Three columns wide. That means *huge*. You'll get a photo credit, too, so readers will know it's your picture."

Straightening the bill in his hands, David let it fall to Ebenezer's desk.

"Not much, considering what they've got. But there it is, Paul. Tomorrow you're a published photographer."

TWELVE

Attack

June 25, 1954

The three-column photograph of Jenny, displayed above the headline *CHICK HOLDS CHICK*, appeared in every edition of the *Mirror*. The picture, as Lena put it, "caused quite a stir." Principal Eleanor Schlee tacked the page to a bulletin board reserved for student achievement.

Bill Moran was charmed. He had Paul's photograph framed. Barbara hung it in the kitchen.

"Terrific work," Bill told Paul. "Do I see a career looming?"

At Paul's house, reaction was mixed.

"It's Stein's doing," George Howland said to Lena, the two sharing lunch on a rainy Sunday afternoon. Paul was across the neighborhood that very moment, developing film in David's darkroom.

George worried about the man–boy friendship. When the two left in David's car for a photo shoot, or spent hours in the darkroom together, George remembered the long-ago incident in Ithaca when agronomy professor Cecil Claire Thatcher tried to fondle him.

He stared at the *Mirror* jump page.

"You think Stein's queer?"

Lena laughed.

"Queer? He dotes on that wife of his! He's always got his arm around what's-her-name. The guy can't keep his hands off her."

Paul's achievement pleased Lena, despite reservations about the girl in the picture.

As for Paul, the satisfaction of taking a fine picture under challenging light conditions made him happy for a few days. Then he turned restless. He wanted to take more portraits. And photograph new landscapes.

Then came a glorious spring morning when Paul and Jenny went to McLean's Farm, where Mary—now in a wheelchair—rolled expertly out to her garden. Jenny brought her lilies and zinnias. Working fast, Paul took ten photographs in less than a minute, among them a picture of Jenny putting a lily in Mary's hair.

That same day, he developed the film unassisted. Borrowing an expression from his mentor, he told Jenny at the bus stop next morning that "exposures in the Mary series are tack-on perfect."

The final weeks of their seventh-grade year passed quickly, and on June 27—one day after leaving Rita Hart's classroom forever—Paul asked Jenny to go with him to Fuller Farm, the run-down place where he'd met and photographed old man Guillermo in November. A view of the brooding West Hills range, glimpsed that day through fog and rain, gnawed at his mind. He had to go back with the Argus.

Jenny yawned into the phone as Paul described the view.

"It's a long walk," she said. "You told me so yourself. It's eighty-six point five degrees in the shade already—I can see the thermometer from where I'm standing—and it's buggy in the woods. Let's go swimming at Clam Shell Beach."

But he held fast to his idea and she relented.

"Okay, I'll go. But come over here first. Mom's giving me a Dorothy Dandridge makeover. Remember her hair? She's the girl in the Tarzan movie."

Half an hour later, Jenny stood in the bright June sun by the edge of the Morans' lawn, hair makeover complete. She twirled in a pirouette when Paul appeared, her long chestnut-brown hair free of braids and swirling like waterfalls.

"See? You are surprised."

She looked older. Like a teenager, he thought.

"You better change into jeans," he said. "The woods near Fuller Farm have briars. You'll be scratched in shorts."

"I'm fine," she said, annoyed because he made no mention of her makeover. And her opinion of Paul didn't improve during the sweaty slog through Mary McLean's easternmost field and a tricky squeeze between barbed-wire strands at the woods line.

"Ouch! Damn-it-all! Looky here at that wire you made me crawl through. It's pulled out half my hair! There's enough hair on that one strand for a bird to build a nest. But you don't care.

"Another thing, Buster. That's not just bittersweet we're walking through. See those shiny leaves of three? You'll be scratching all night. I will too. You and your damn brainstorms. We could be swimming at Clam Shell right now."

When they reached the outermost pasture of Fuller Farm, they paused at a rotted wood fence. Before them a close-cropped pasture rose to a ridge where six cows grazed. Beyond the ridge, several miles distant, the purple-blue West Hills rose from the flat Long Island landscape. The ridge interested Jenny.

"We ought to ride our bikes there sometime," she said. "Then hike Jayne's Hill!"

So taken were they with the view that neither saw Eddie Fuller approach catlike along the rotten fence line.

Then, in surprise and fear, Jenny drew in her breath as Eddie Fuller—Eduardo, the farm workers called him—pointed a thick finger at Paul.

"You're the one took pictures of my boys last year. Don't do it again, you hear? I pay them to work. What do you think they are, movie stars? They're not here now anyway."

Despite the heat, Eddie Fuller wore a red wool shirt and army fatigues tucked into black boots: the same clothes he'd worn in November. The man was amazingly tall. Six foot three, Paul thought. No. More like six and a half feet. A shiny gray scar ran across his forehead, the top of the scar partly hidden by a cowboy hat. The healed wound reminded Paul of something Guillermo had said about Fuller.

"Crazy from war. Crazy at Guadalcanal." He'd also mentioned a "Battle at Bloody Ridge."

Fuller's cranky nature didn't discourage Paul. He studied the farmer's statue-like cattle a hundred feet away—foreground to the photograph he planned to take. Emboldened by eagerness, he had no fear of the giant farmer.

"I didn't come to take pictures of your workmen," he said. "I'd like to photograph your cows on the ridge and the hills beyond. It's a nice view."

"Nice view," Fuller mimicked, imitating a woman's voice. "Nice view, my ass. I'm selling this place and going to Florida. Going to get me a woman. Like that one there."

The farmer stared at Jenny, who looked away.

"Climb the ridge and take all the pictures you want, sonny."

"Hey," Fuller continued, eyes on Jenny, "you take pictures, too?"

She shook her head.

"While he's out there with the cows, I'll show you my heifers. Baby calves, you'd call them. Born in May. They're in my milk house behind the barn."

Jenny put her index finger to her lips. Paul, composing in his mind the picture he intended to take, turned to climb the ridge.

"Go ahead, Jenny. I won't be long."

"Sure. You go up there," Fuller said. "Take all the pictures you want."

Raising a large hand, he motioned Jenny to follow him. "You and me. We see the calves."

When Paul reached the height of land, the view of the West Hills was everything he had hoped for. Cumulus clouds turning to thunderheads were a bonus, and he reached for the yellow cloud filter David had bought in the city. He was pushing the filter onto the Argus lens when he heard a muffled scream.

Jenny!

Dropping the camera, he descended the ridge at a dead run. He rounded the barn, then sprinted for the milk house, Jenny's panicked screams now loud in his ears.

"You creep! You bastard! Get away from me!"

Paul threw himself against the milk house door. It didn't move. He pulled its brass handle. Nothing happened. Stepping back, his cries and screams now mingling with Jenny's, Paul grabbed a nail-studded two-by-four and smashed every window above the milk house door. Shattered glass rained down on his wrists and arms, which quickly turned slippery with blood.

Inside the cement-floored building, Jenny backed away from Fuller, desperately dodging his violent lunges.

"You fucking vixen!" he yelled. "Get on that floor. Now! Or I'll hit you so hard you won't wake up for a month of Sundays."

He caught her once, but she broke free. Her blouse hung in shreds. Backing away from her enemy, Jenny's peripheral vision landed on a bucket of syringes, each one armed with a long hypodermic needle.

Stooping, she grabbed a syringe by its shaft just as Fuller—diving for her legs—sent her sprawling on the floor. Pinning her with his knees, he ripped at her shorts.

In that instant, she jabbed the hypodermic needle into his right eye.

*   *   *

During the days that followed, Jenny made clear she did not aim to take out Fuller's eye. "He was trying to rape me," she told the first detective to interview her. "He was tearing at my clothes and weaving his head around. I struck for his face. The needle hit his eye."

Fuller bellowed like a wounded animal. He staggered to his feet while his blood spurted onto the glass-littered floor. Jenny rushed to the door but couldn't get it open. It was Fuller, still screaming in pain, who finally lifted and dropped the massive plank that held it shut.

Jenny was first out of the building. Running to Paul, she grabbed his hand. They turned to see Eddy Fuller stumbling side to side in front of the cave-like milk house—his one good eye staring at them in hatred.

"You," he growled. "You're worse than the fucking Japs. And you're good as dead."

Lifting a cement block from the ground as if it were weightless, he threw it at them. The block sailed over Paul's head and knocked a branch off a tree. Paul and Jenny turned and ran as stones and boulders rained down around them. They kept going until they were deep within the bittersweet-tangled forest.

Minutes had passed since they'd last heard Fuller scream.

They stopped.

Jenny faced Paul, her scratched and bleeding face tense with fury. "You brought me to that place. And then—oh, my God—you left me with a monster!"

They cried, Paul repeating that he was sorry, yet knowing even as he spoke that the apology was meaningless next to the enormity of Jenny's distress. After a while, they stood silent, glancing now and then in the direction of Fuller Farm.

No one had followed.

Jenny tore a strip of cloth from her shredded blouse. This she ran through two belt loops and cinched it tight to keep her shorts in place.

"Did he rape you?"

"No."

"You're spattered with blood."

"His," she said.

Exhausted, they walked to the end of the woods and continued on to Jenny's house. Barbara Moran shrieked when she saw her daughter through the screen door. She ushered them into the kitchen. Then, partway through Jenny's explanation, she lifted the wall phone from its hook and—with tears running down her face—told the operator to ring Crystal Police. "Emergency number please."

Within minutes the Moran driveway filled with vehicles: an ambulance from Crystal General, a police car with two officers, Bill Moran's car, and, shortly afterwards, a second Crystal Police cruiser driven by a balding detective. All seven occupants of the cars and ambulance, among them a red-haired nurse named Irma, crowded into the Morans' house.

Paul, asked to wait outdoors, sat on the open stucco porch. He heard pieces of conversation from the house. He held his hands to his ears when Jenny sobbed.

Eventually the nurse and ambulance driver left in their vehicle. The detective came out on the porch and sat next to Paul. He leaned against the redwood siding as Paul did, the two resting their eyes on the leafy woods.

"Cool out here," the policeman said at length.

He half turned to face Paul and extended his hand. Hesitantly, Paul shook it.

"Joe Beasley's the name. I help Crystal Police with some investigations. And I'd like you to tell me everything that happened this morning, starting with your departure from this house at, I believe, eight thirty."

In a low, sometimes trembling voice, Paul did as he was told until he came to the part of the story where he'd left Jenny alone with Fuller.

"I'm sorry," he sobbed, covering his face with his hands.

Joe Beasley dropped his scribbled notes on the stucco floor. "You feel bad because you didn't protect Miss Moran?"

Paul nodded, crying as he told the detective that he could have stopped the attack if he'd stayed with her.

"Son," the detective said, putting his hand on Paul's shoulder, "the mistake you and Jenny made was going to that farm in the first place. And yes, you should have stayed with her. But listen carefully: You could not have stopped that monster. If you'd tried, he would have hurt you. Or worse. You understand?"

He did, and was thankful to have Joe Beasley at his side.

By late afternoon, the last police car had left the Moran drive. Paul—worried about Jenny but hesitant to go inside—paced the lawn. Cicadas sang in the woods. His arm, lacerated earlier in the day by falling glass, throbbed in spite of pain medicine and black-thread stitches Bill Moran used to close the cut .

When the porch door made a latch-spring sound, Paul turned and saw Bill beckoning him inside.

He found Jenny eating Wheaties in the kitchen.

"Weird supper, Jen," her mother said as she rinsed spoons and cups, dishtowel thrown back on her shoulder. "You could have had chicken or beef stew. Foods more supper-ish."

"It's what I feel like eating," Jenny replied. "Breakfast in reverse. Hi, Paul."

There was forced cheerfulness in their voices. Other than that, it was life as usual in the Morans' kitchen, and Paul was relieved. Jenny's hair was back in braids, revealing a nasty black-and-blue bruise on her cheek. She told him that her mom had already fed the Reds, so he didn't have to. She wasn't allowed outside, she explained, at least for now.

"How's that arm?" Bill asked Paul.

Paul signaled okay with a thumbs-up.

"You should go home soon," the doctor said. "You've been away a long time and your parents will worry. But hold on one second. I'm going to call your mom and explain things so you don't have to."

*   *   *

The doctor closed the door to his office and, using his desk phone, summarized for Lana the day's events.

"There are things Paul and Jenny don't know," he told her, "and I suggest you do not bring them up. Eddy Fuller was arrested at Crystal General for assault, battery, and attempted rape. He'd driven himself to the hospital, claiming to have poked his eye with a sewing needle while mending pants. And another thing you should know: He's going to be charged tomorrow with the murder of Pricilla Rand, the sixteen-year-old polio victim who disappeared a year ago. You may remember the case from stories in the newspaper and WGCM broadcast alerts. She was last seen in her wheelchair on the Oak Grove Road that runs by Fuller Farm."

He paused while Lena asked a question.

"Fuller is implicated by clothes that police found in the room where Jenny was attacked."

Lena wanted to know why a farmer would keep hypodermic needles in a barn.

"For mastitis," he explained, beginning to lose patience. "A bovine disease. But don't mention that or anything else I've told you to anyone, including Paul. He's exhausted. Give him a couple of aspirin if the laceration I told you about bothers him."

He slammed the phone onto its receiver. Three sheets to the wind, he thought. He pursed his mouth. There was nothing he could do about that.

By eight o'clock, Jenny and her parents were sick of the subject that had altered their lives. Jenny took a second shower. She rearranged her bureau-top doll collection and fell asleep in minutes. Then, sometime after midnight, she dreamt it was spring and she was running with Paul through familiar woods blanketed with mayflowers. Familiar except for black holes in the earth. But they were easy to avoid by jumping left or right. Then suddenly she was falling down and down in darkness. She awoke screaming, the room lights on and her mother shaking her gently.

"It was so horrible," she sobbed.

Barbara spoke soothingly as she crawled into the narrow bed, arms around her daughter. They slept through the rest of the night, awaking to bright sunlight.

THIRTEEN

Healing

August 1, 1954

Throughout the hot summer, Jenny had recurring nightmares. Her parents rarely slept through the night. When Bill awoke from his own disturbing dreams, he'd find Barbara staring at the ceiling. If Barbara was first to jolt awake, there was her sleepless husband. Not once had they considered such a terrible possibility. Their daughter was thirteen. In the Bronx, crimes like this happened—or in the Chicago slums.

But not in Crystal.

Yet it had.

During those sleepless nights, Bill Moran imagined states and towns where a family could live in safety.

* * *

Jenny had changed. She was too quiet. Always watchful. Inclined to look over her shoulder. Her parents feared it was permanent.

She spent hours in her room reading book after book: *Lad, a Dog*, *The Call of the Wild*, and *Luckiest Girl*. Mornings and evenings, she left the house briefly to walk the half-mile Sylvan Road circle, but never alone. She wanted her parents with her and they always obliged.

Jenny's choice of clothes troubled Bill and Barbara. She wore long pants and long-sleeved shirts every day, even when the thermometer passed ninety. At Jenny's request, Barbara cut her hair twice in July and put what remained in tiny pigtails. "I want them like I had in first grade," she told her mother. "Remember first grade with nice Mrs. Nelson? We napped on the floor after lunch, each of us on a little mat."

Two days after the incident, Bill Moran arranged twice-weekly appointments for Jenny with his psychiatrist friend, Dr. Joel Zalerin in Roslyn. And he took a one-month emergency leave from Crystal Clinic.

"I'll use my vacation to get Mom's Lightning out of the boatyard and onto its mooring," he announced over breakfast on the first day of his work-free month.

"But before we move the boat," he continued, "we'll build that big wire chicken run you've been campaigning for, Jenny. Then those hens of yours can stretch their legs safe from foxes and weasels."

"They're called pullets, Dad," she said. "They're not officially hens until they're a year old. But I like your idea. My poor birds have been trapped for weeks in that grubby barn. When do we start?"

"Fifteen minutes, I'd say. Crystal Lumber delivered fencing and posts yesterday, and I've asked Paul to help. He'll be here in a minute."

With Bill pounding posts into the woodsy earth and his two assistants stapling wire, they finished the chicken run in two days. It was twenty-five feet wide and seventy feet long. Enclosed within the rectangle were three sugar maples, a grove of mountain laurel, and a patch of sweet fern. "The Reds' Ritz," Bill said as the three of them watched Jenny's half-grown pullets scratch for worms in the leafy underbrush.

A week later, Art Spirit floated at its orange mooring off Clam Shell Beach. The Lightning had a new jib and spinnaker, its red hull freshly painted at Crystal Yachts. Then, on a weather-perfect day, all four took their first sail of the season.

"I'm sure the two of you could handle it alone," Barbara said. "But there's a freshening breeze this morning and you'll need our adult weight to keep Art Spirit mast-up."

"You and Dad getting a bit porky, Mom?" Jenny replied, smiling for the first time in weeks.

"Them's fighting words!" Barbara shot back, raising her hand in mock fury.

And she was happy because it seemed to her in that moment that the darkness surrounding them them had finally departed. But later, when the day turned hot and Jenny took off her polo shirt, it pained Barbara to see scars where Fuller's nails had raked her neck and back.

The summer sun shone warm and glorious never the less as they sailed the Lightning past the last headland and far into Long Island Sound. Before coming about, they sailed close enough to the Connecticut shore to see architectural detail adorning nineteenth-century mansions.

"It is so peaceful," Jenny said. "I wish this day—this afternoon—would last forever."

After that day, more progress followed.

"So what did you and Dr. Zalerin talk about today?" Barbara asked two days later as Jenny jumped from her dad's car. It was a ritual question Barbara asked each time her daughter returned from a Dr. Zalerin appointment.

Jenny's response was always the same: "Classified information, Mrs. Moran."

This time Jenny broke the script.

"Actually, we didn't talk about anything," she told her mother. "We played Scrabble twice and I beat him twice. The best thing was, I know he was trying!"

That evening, as Paul and Jenny walked the Sylvan Circle, the change in Jenny's manner gave him courage to ask the question he hadn't dared voice.

"When we went on that walk last June…you know the one. What I'd like to know is, did you have Mary's amethyst stone?"

Jenny walked faster. She looked into the woods, then back at him.

She was annoyed.

"What do you think I am, superstitious? Why in hell do you bring that up?"

"I'm sorry," he said. "But it's been on my mind. The stone is supposed to bring luck. And it did for a while. You won the spelling bee. You got the baby chicks. *The Mirror* ran the photograph I took of you holding the chick, like the stone's luck rubbed off on me. So why…why didn't it protect you?"

They walked on in silence that was not uncomfortable.

"The amethyst stone does bring luck," Jenny said at length. "Of that I'm certain. But it won't protect you from harm. Or sorrow."

She made him promise to never again mention the attack.

But a minute later it was Jenny who returned to the subject she'd banned.

"In thinking about it, maybe—just maybe—the amethyst stone did protect me. Eddie Fuller is sentenced to a life term in Sing-Sing. He'll die there. And here we are walking the Sylvan Circle. Is that just chance or fate? I think it's the amethyst stone."

*　　*　　*

As summer went on, Paul rarely thought about his beloved Argus, dropped weeks before on Eddie Fuller's land. Not once did he question Detective Beasley's warning to stay away from Fuller Farm. His camera—rained upon by now, probably trampled by cows—was ruined anyway.

So much had happened that the loss of the camera didn't bother him. David's reaction did. Sooner or later, he knew, David would invite him on a picture-taking adventure—or ask why he no longer visited. And what would he say? The predicament made his heart race, and he resolved to face the dilemma before David's inevitable phone call.

So early one Sunday, Paul wheeled his black Raleigh three-speed out of the cellar, noting as he did the white dust that had settled on its fenders. No surprise there, or in the fact that both tires needed air. Unlike every other summer, when he and Jenny had biked the country roads, they'd quit after the June incident. How different this summer had been.

And he tensed thinking of the errand ahead.

Paul found David high up on a wooden extension ladder, brushing blue paint on clapboards at the peak of his house.

"Paul!" he yelled, turning as he did, right hand gripping the highest ladder rung, his left holding a brush that dripped blue splotches onto the pebble drive below. "We must have ESP or something. I'd planned to call you this afternoon. What's happened? You fall off the earth?"

Carefully, David descended, still talking. "I've got something really important to tell you," he said, placing his brush in a turpentine-filled bucket as he stepped from the ladder. "Remember those negatives you left here in May? I processed them of course. They're shots of your girlfriend helping Mary McLean in her garden. Mary's aged a lot. I see she's in a wheelchair. And I got to thinking. Her land was Crystal's last dairy farm. As far as I can tell, there's no more than a dozen farms left in all of Suffolk County—most of them on the east end. Farming defined life here before the war. Dairy and potatoes. That was Long Island. Now it's almost gone."

As he rinsed the paintbrush, pausing to wipe smudges of blue from his wrist and fingers, David told Paul he'd floated the idea of a "Last Dairy" story to *The Mirror* feature editor, Mike Britain, and that Mike had "snapped it up in a heartbeat."

"'Stein,'" Mike says to me, 'this is exactly what we need. The publisher's thirsty for this kind of stuff. Readers love it. I'll put Clyde Benson on the story and you tell that kid to do the photos.'

"Then Mike went on about his problems. 'Photogs are spread too thin, Davy, as you well know. They can't do the whole damn island. They're stretched just covering the boroughs.'"

Now David looked at Paul, his eyes glimmering with enthusiasm.

"The upshot is, Clyde's going to meet you at Mary's Tuesday at four o'clock. The forecast is good. Light should be perfect."

Paul drew in his breath. "Something happened," he said. And told David the story.

"I deserve to have lost the Argus," he concluded. "I left Jenny alone when she needed me."

Had Paul been less focused on his story, he would have noticed the slump in David's shoulders and the gray cast to his face.

"I…read that story in the *Long Islander*. It was in *The Mirror* too. Not once—never—did it occur to me that the 'two juveniles' described in the papers were you and Jenny."

David brought his hands to his temples and, dropping his head to his knees, stared at the paint-spattered pebbles. When he raised his head, Paul was crying.

"Listen," David said. "Look at me now. This is important. You need to understand that you are not responsible for Eddie Fuller attacking Jenny. Evil—and that man is evil—disarms victims with stealth. How could you possibly have guessed Eddie Fuller's motive when he invited Jenny to see some calves? Listen! Rachel's grandparents lived in Berlin before the war. Aaron Goodman ran a jewelry store. It had been in his family three generations. People loved Aaron. He had a watch repair contract with the German army, for God sakes.

"So when the hatred began, Aaron didn't think he was in danger. He sent his wife and daughter to Brooklyn to wait out the trouble. Aaron died at Dachau.

"You see what I'm saying? Evil's approach is silent. You didn't know how sick Eddie Fuller is. And don't forget that you may have saved

Jenny's life by smashing the milk house windows. You distracted the son-of-a-bitch. That gave Jenny the chance to strike."

Though he meant what he said and was pleased to see the effect of his words on Paul, David's opinion of his adopted town spiraled down. For he'd imagined—before Paul's disclosure of the Fuller incident—that Crystal was nearly exempt from the mayhem that defined New York City. In fact, he'd imagined an invisible protective line running north to south through the Queens County town of Sunnyside. West of Sunnyside were gangland slayings and random murder, the aftermath of which he photographed weekly. East of the line, quietly settled in laurel and oak forests, civilized people lived.

Or so he'd thought.

All Pollyanna nonsense, he concluded. Crystal, thirty-five miles from the city line, differed only in degree. In his mind, David began a slow separation from the town he had once adored. Was there a better place? Maybe not. But he would search.

He looked at Paul.

"We've got to replace the Argus. That's the order of the day. Clyde's counting on you to shoot the McLean feature Tuesday, and trust me—you don't want to disappoint Clyde."

Late the following evening, David's sedan kicked up cinder dust as it fast-braked on the Howlands' drive. Rinsing dishes at the sink, George Howland peered through the kitchen casement.

"Goddamned guy drives like a punk," he muttered.

Paul ran to the car.

"It's not spiffy new like the other," David said as he opened the car door and handed Paul a tired-looking camera with nicks and dings. "But don't underestimate it just because it looks beat-up. It's got a clean lens and its shutter's on the money. I got it from Sam Goldenthall. He owns Goldenthall Camera on Forty-Second Street. Sam's a reconditioning genius and he swears by this C-4 Argus.

"Take this cloud filter and three rolls of Tri-X," David continued, handing Paul a paper bag. "Bring Jenny when you meet Clyde. Mike Britain wants shots of her interacting with Mary. Do close-ups of them both. Remember to bracket exposures above and below your meter reading. And don't forget the point of Clyde's story: the final days of a once-thriving dairy."

To the surprise of everyone including Clyde Benson, the photo shoot and interview went off problem-free. Weather was precisely what Paul had hoped for, the sky milky overcast with afternoon sun strong enough to cast shadows.

Three days later—the double-page feature spread on Barbara Moran's table—Paul studied his photographs surrounded by print. Most prominent was a close-up of Jenny with a huge bunch of calendulas intended for Mary's lap. Their eyes met in the photograph, the wheelchair-bound woman extending a gnarled hand toward the flowers.

A second picture had Jenny pushing Mary's wheelchair close by the big barn, Mary looking content, her black cane resting across the wheelchair rails. Largest of the three photographs was a shot Paul had taken from the peak of the barn roof. Prominent in the image was the crisscross pattern of split rail fences running through fields, the distant West Hills at the skyline.

Final Days for Crystal's Last Farm was the banner headline.

Later, sitting in the laurel bushes, Jenny read the story to Paul, including what Clyde had quoted her as saying about the farm: "I wish it could stay this way forever. Beautiful like it is this afternoon."

"Did you really say that?" Paul asked, "I mean, those exact words?"

"'Course I did," she replied, poking him in the ribs. "Clyde Benson wrote down everything. He took notes with a red mechanical pencil on brown paper folded over backwards. I watched him. Clyde's got terrible handwriting."

It was a bittersweet moment for Paul. He loved being close to Jenny, the two of them sitting Indian-fashion under the green laurel while Jenny read in her bell-clear voice. But as he listened, anxieties took his spirit down. Is there anything more ridiculous, he wondered, than a newspaper photographer who can't read?

He went on to qualify his self-damnation. He could read some road signs. But that was small consolation for a thirteen-year-old going into eighth grade.

Depression dogged him that night and into the next day, even as he rowed the Morans' dingy to *Art Spirit* for a final summer sail. Jenny took the stern seat, the dinghy's bow piled high with canvas, batons, life preservers, and the makings of lunch.

Twenty minutes later they had mainsail and jib raised. At the tiller, Jenny tacked sharply into the wind. Her contented smile bothered Paul, who felt anything but content.

"School starts in two days, you know," he said.

She went on smiling.

"Why so chipper?"

Jenny glanced at the masthead where the Lightning's jib and mainsail formed white triangles against the sky.

"I just love being alive."

FOURTEEN

Breakthrough

December 27, 1954

It was Jenny's idea.

"Guess what!" she shouted into the phone. "Wilhoite Pond's frozen. It's half a mile of black ice. Mom and I drove by it this morning on our way to the *Nutcracker* ballet. What say we walk there? Today. This afternoon. You bring your new Christmas skates. Me? I bring my Christmas skis to try out on the hill in back of the pond. So what do you think? We walk to the pond. You skate. I ski. We hoof it home by dark."

Paul smiled, telephone receiver to his ear.

"Terrific idea!"

Everything in the last four months had been terrific.

His run of luck had started in September when Eva Christy, walking into her eighth-grade room the first day of school, locked eyes with him.

"Paul. Paul Howland," she said. "I can't tell you how happy I am to be your teacher! To think, I finally have Paul the photographer in my class."

Surprises followed surprises that morning.

"It's a nice day," Mrs. Christy said, after taking attendance. "Too nice to be indoors. So I'll read to you under the linden tree."

"Crackpot," Fran Bajkowski whispered to Katherine Kimberly. "We have a crackpot teacher."

Katherine clamped her wrist to her mouth to stifle laughter.

But when they gathered beneath the dark-leafed tree that first day of school, the solemnity quieted even the silliest.

"The title of our book," Eva Christy began, her gray eyes sweeping their faces, is *Boy on Horseback*. It's by Lincoln Steffens, and it's an autobiography. An autobiography is a true story about an author's life. In this case, about Lincoln Steffens's boyhood in Sacramento, California.

"'I began riding alone,'" Mrs. Christy read. "'When I mounted my pony...I had a world before me. I felt lifted up to another plane, with a wider range. I could explore regions I had not been able to reach on foot.'"

In Paul's mind, the words evoked a river of images. The linden tree and September grass ceased to exist. It was 1900. He was in Sacramento, where boys galloped past sagebrush and farms in a land just emerged from pioneer days.

The magic went on. There was no homework for Paul or the other one-time Butterflies. In a letter to Paul's mother, Eva Christy told Lena she would assign no homework to her son.

"My goal, dear Lena," the letter concluded, "is to make this year a happy one for Paul. Please be my accomplice in this endeavor.

"Your friend, Eva Christy."

Books appeared on the desk Paul shared with Jenny. The first was about coastal schooners, its pages illustrated with lavish black-and-white photographs.

But he still didn't read and at times felt disconsolate. Eva Christy had tried. Why couldn't he learn?

❊　　❊　　❊

"Hey!" Jenny yelled, turning onto the narrow snowy path descending to Wilhoite Pond. "How come you're going slow? All you've got to carry are skates. And here I'm lugging my whole ski outfit and out ahead."

"Just thinking about school," he said.

"Stop thinking. We've got seven days' vacation."

They continued down the snow-slippery path to the pond. Jenny talked about her family. "Like I was telling you at the house," she said, "we all have skis now. My mom's are like mine. Dad has blue Kneissl skis. In March he's taking us to Cannon Mountain in New Hampshire for a week of skiing. My Dad is nuts about New Hampshire. He went to a medical school at Dartmouth. New Hampshire, New Hampshire, New Hampshire. It's all he talks about."

Before them the path widened, then ended by a snowbank at the edge of Willhoite Pond Road. Directly across the seldom-used roadway, black ice glinted in the sun. Jenny was right, Paul thought. It was perfect for skating.

Robert and Beth Wilhoite had made their big pond in 1935 by impounding Moffat Mill Stream. A year later, five contractors built the Wilhoite's Federalist-style mansion on a wooded hillside above the pond. There were other great houses in this part of Crystal, known locally as The Heights. But unlike most of their neighbors, the Wilhoites did not surround their property with a cyclone fence.

They enjoyed seeing skaters on the pond. Elderly Robert Wilhoite, an import–export banker who commuted to New York until he was seventy-five, kept a pair of binoculars by his living room chair. With them he watched skaters far below: skillful adults inscribing figure eights, hands clasped behind their backs, teenagers cracking the whip, moms shepherding children who wobbled on double runners.

Opening their pond to skaters wasn't all the Wilhoites did for Crystal. Once a year in August, they invited townspeople to their private freshwater beach, its white sand trucked in from dunes fronting Long Island Sound. The couple further pleased their guests by providing hamburgers, soda, and corn on the cob. Robert Wilhoite went so far as to hire lifeguards to watch the swimmers on Wilhoite Beach Day.

*   *   *

"You see that chute up there between the trees—that place on the hillside below the estate? That's where I'm going to ski."

Jenny put on her boots and skies and poled toward the pond's earthen dam.

Paul kicked off his rubber boots and pulled on his new skates. A thunder-like boom out on the pond reassured him that the ice was safe—it was expanding.

He turned toward Jenny's departing figure, now a hundred feet away. "Hey!" he yelled. "Where is everyone? There should be tons of kids on a day like this."

Jenny stopped. She spoke through cupped hands. "Too damn lazy," she yelled back. "They're home watching the Buster Brown Afternoon Special."

Paul laced his skates and, pushing off as he'd done hundreds of times before on his old hockey skates, fell flat on his face. He stood and touched his gloved hand to his nose. No blood. That was a good thing. It was his fault, he realized. He'd forgotten the trip-up points on the tip of figure skate blades. He pushed off again, this time keeping his weight on the flat midsection of the blades.

Quickly, he gathered speed. He was careful. Figure skates had a life of their own.

For the second time, the sonic boom of expanding ice sounded. The thundering noise and gleam of sun on the pond—these and a new sense of competency buoyed his spirit. Paul let the tip of one skate drag lightly so it caught the ice and flung him around a hundred and eighty degrees. And he flew backwards down the pond before quick-turning to regain forward progress. He tried grinding the bar, and was thrilled when he inscribed a tight circle simply by crossing one foot in front of the other.

From the corner of his vision he saw Jenny on her skis poling over the ice in front of the dam.

In a moment he'd skate to her. But first he'd attempt a figure eight. Concentrating on his blades, Paul completed the move perfectly. Was Jenny watching? Straightening, he squinted through white glare to the far end of the lake.

Nothing. Where was she, anyway?

Then he detected movement, something small and green moving at ice level by the dam.

Jenny's mitten!

And instantly he knew that Jenny had gone through the ice, skis attached to her boots and pole straps looped to her wrists. He pushed off hard toward the dam, forgetting in panic the quirks of his skates. He fell hard on his face—got up—and skated on. Though he moved faster than he'd ever gone on skates, his progress seemed agonizingly slow.

Jenny's strangled cries grew louder.

Sliding on his knees to the broken ice edge, Paul grasped her out-stretched hand and pulled. Her head and shoulders rose from the icy slurry, then fell back. In his hand was a green mitten.

He lunged again, this time grabbing her wrist. With his free hand, he slid the ski pole strap from her wrist. Seconds later and he had her other hand free.

All the time she screamed, "The skis! My skis! They're pulling me down!"

Flattening himself stomach-down on the ice—his face beneath dark water—Paul reached down and down until he had her ski binding in hand. He jerked it free and, in the same manner, removed the second ski.

"Climb out!" he shouted. "Move it. Now!"

She couldn't. Cold had taken her strength and focus. Instead of squirming onto solid ice, she broke small pieces of ice from the edge of the gaping hole and dropped them in the water one by one.

Paul screamed in helplessness, then remembered the parka's cinch belt at Jenny's waist. Lying flat on the wet ice, he reached for her belt, found it, and pulled as hard as he could.

But instead of pulling Jenny from the water, ice beneath him gave way.

He threw his body left so as not to fall on top of her, landing hard and going down in darkness before managing to kick and turn toward light.

And as he struggled in the deep water, one skate blade struck a sunken log. He jammed the other blade into the wood and stood half out of the water.

Again he grasped Jenny's parka belt. And pulled and then pushed with all this strength until she slid onto solid ice beyond the break. When she hunched up and crawled, he knew she was safe.

Now he had to get out. But his thoughts were a jumble. He stood paralyzed, as if in a nightmare. Then he saw Jenny inching toward him. She paused three feet from the hole, her face white as paper, strands of brown hair frozen to her cheeks.

Then he saw the ski pole in Jenny's hand—basket end extended toward him. He grasped it and pulled just hard enough to bring his right leg onto solid ice and roll out.

They crawled to snow-covered ground by the pond's edge. Paul saw his dry boots two feet away and, in a deranged hypothermic state, it seemed remarkable to him to be sitting next to boots he'd taken off to go skating. And how long ago was that? Days? Weeks? Everything was strange now. The pond swayed. The sun went out.

✳   ✳   ✳

He heard an adult voice, opened his eyes, and saw an elderly woman. Her white hair blew in the wind. Pink slippers covered her bare feet.

"Stand up," she ordered, pulling both of them to their feet and herding them like stumbling beasts to a car with a broken headlight and crashed-in fender.

They sat side by side in the car's backseat. And Paul knew that the woman in the blue robe and pink slippers was Beth Wilhoite, the same Beth Wilhoite who barbecued hamburgers at the summer picnic. Now she leaned over Jenny, shaking her so hard that the girl's head wobbled.

"No, you can't sleep," Mrs. Wilhoite scolded. "Not yet. Not until we get to the hospital."

Then they bounced down pothole-filled Wilhoite Road in a car that seemed to be flying.

"Where are you taking us?"

Jenny was wide awake now and leaning forward, muddy hands clutching the back of Mrs. Wilhoite's seat.

"Where?" she demanded.

The elderly woman sat bolt upright in the driver's seat looking straight through her windshield, hands gripping the gray steering wheel.

"You're going to the hospital. West Crystal Community."

"No," Jenny said, her voice loud. She never spoke like that, Paul thought. Not to adults.

Heat flowed from the dark space beneath the front seat. Paul watched muddy water course down his jacket onto Mrs. Wilhoite's flower-printed seat cover. Jenny's hands continued to grip Mrs. Wilhoite's front seat, the girl's mud-stained nails inches from Mrs. Wilhoite's hair.

"Please drive us to my house," Jenny said, her voice calm now. "My dad's a doctor. We don't need to go to the hospital."

In the car mirror, Paul saw the reflection of Mrs. Wilhoite's face. The woman looked at Jenny through the same mirror.

"Your father's name?"

When Jenny replied, mentioning Bill Moran's clinic, too, Paul felt the car slow.

"Sylvan Road?" Mrs. Wilhoite asked.

Jenny nodded. Brakes squealed, the force of the near-instant stop slamming the two backseat passengers against each other.

"We'll have you there in a jiffy," Mrs. Wilhoite said, eyeing them again in the car mirror. "You two seem to be on the mend."

When the big car reached the paved road, they drove for a while in silence while Beth Wilhoite alternately watched the road and observed her passengers.

"I'll say one good thing for this Cadillac," she said, "it has a good heater. Poor car. I drove it smack-dab into the stone wall next to that infernally steep driveway of ours. Of course, I was going too fast—hightailing it down to the pond and thinking the worst every inch of the way. You can thank Bob that you're alive. He spotted the two of you through his binoculars, struggling down by the dam."

In the car mirror, Paul saw her expression change.

"What on earth were you thinking? Three days ago the pond was open water. Three days! It takes longer than that to freeze so it's safe for skating. And it never does freeze by the dam.

"Anyway," Bob rushed to my dressing room, where I was putting on my face for the Crystal Garden Club luncheon. I thought Bob was having apoplexy. He dragged me to the living room window. That's when I ran out and crashed my car."

Minutes later, the Cadillac bounced to a stop in the Morans' drive. Beth Wilhoite, agile for a woman over seventy, leapt from the car to help Jenny from the backseat.

By the time the three reached the house, Barbara Moran was fully in charge.

"Jenny," she said, "into the front hall bathroom. Beth—kindly put Jenny in the shower clothes and all. Water warm but not hot. Watch that she stays conscious. I'll be there in a second."

Paul felt Mrs. Moran's arm on his shoulder. "You have the bedroom shower," she said, leading him to a yellow-tiled bath. He watched her turn faucets.

"Careful," she said, helping him over the edge of the tub until he stood dead center under warm water that beat upon his jacket with the sound of rain. She helped him unzip his parka, and threw it in a heap on the bathroom floor.

"Stand there until you're warm. Then take off those muddy clothes! I'll leave one of Bill's shirts and a pair of trousers by the door."

When Paul walked into the kitchen twenty minutes later, fully dressed and warm, Jenny laughed.

"Dad's shrunk," she said.

She sat cross-legged on a bench by the table, head wrapped turban style in a white bath towel. She wore a red plaid bathrobe buttoned to the neck.

Barbara Moran, pouring cocoa into four red cups, glanced at her daughter.

"That's a summer bathrobe you're wearing," she said, pulling a heavy yellow coat from the kitchen closet and draping it around Jenny's shoulders.

"Mom. Please. I'm boiling already."

Beth Wilhoite, still in her blue robe and slippers, perched on a stool in a corner of the kitchen. She was clearly enjoying herself. For a long while no one spoke.

It was Barbara who broke the silence.

"So Miss Jenny—about that note. You said you were going to ski while Paul skated. No mention as to where. So I assumed of course that you went to McLean's Pond where the water's all of two feet deep."

She glanced at Paul, then back to Jenny.

"You could have died. Both of you."

"We'll close the gate," Beth said, "and keep it closed until the ice is solid. Kids can walk around the gate anyway because the property isn't fenced. But a closed gate sends a message. And I'll have Bob put up a sign."

They ate crackers with peanut butter and there was no more discussion of the pond. Jenny chatted about soon-to-begin dance lessons at school. Barbara washed and dried their soaked clothing. She loaned Paul rubber boots for the walk home.

He said good-bye and thanked Jenny's mom and Beth Wilhoite, and shut the porch door quietly behind him. It was nearly dark out, light snow sifting down. For a moment he stood on the Morans' porch watching the white flakes fall to earth.

When the door latch clicked, he turned and saw Jenny standing near. She'd thrown on the yellow coat, her feet still in slippers. She brought her index finger to her lips.

"My mother will kill me if she finds I'm out."

Her eyes looked past him to the woods.

"Snowing," she said, her voice hardly more than a whisper.

Stepping closer, she turned and faced him.

"I couldn't get out. You saved my life."

"Well," he said, "you gave me the ski pole and held tight when I needed something to hold. I guess we saved each other."

Her hair brushed his face as she kissed him. She stepped back, her hand on the doorknob.

"I love you, Paul."

*   *   *

Six days later, on a Monday morning, Paul began to read. Nothing about the day's beginning prepared him for such an astonishing event. For months afterwards, he thought about the first hours of that day, breaking each hour into pieces as he searched for some clue to explain what happened. But he could think of none.

It was eleven o'clock and Mrs. Christy was at the blackboard writing white chalk words she separated with perpendicular lines, talking while she wrote about an adverbial subordinate clause. It meant nothing to him, and that didn't matter because Mrs. Christy excused him from board work. He was free to look at books she left on his desk. There was a new one that morning about lions.

Paul opened the book to its center, where there was a picture of a mother lion leading her cubs out of the jungle into a field. His eyes focused on a block of print at the top of the page. And he read:

Never before had Simba explored the world beyond the den where he was born. But this morning, as he wrestled with his brothers and sisters on the sandy earth by the cave that was his home, Simba knew the day would different. So when he heard his mother the Lioness growl and walk to the edge of a prairie he had never before explored, he followed her into the unknown, pleased to see his brothers and sisters trotting along beside as the lion family walked for the first time onto the plains of Serengeti. How the wet grass tickled his stomach! How large the palm trees grew off to one side! Entering the prairie just like his family, he saw a second lioness leading her pride. Simba was happy. This was his first hunt.

Slowly, Paul slid the lion book toward Jenny's side of the desk. More slowly still, he drew the thick red-covered photography book that Eva Christy had put by the lion story. With his thumb on the book's spine, he opened to a random page.

Every point of every natural object sends out rays of light in all directions, and in ordinary photographic work those rays...

This was wonderful, yet frightening! He glanced up from his book, aware that he no longer heard Mrs. Christy's voice. Then their eyes met and he saw that she looked at him in a questioning way.

Paul nodded. And he saw the trace of a smile on her lips as she turned back to the board to write a sentence intersected with lines.

He felt his face going red, and to keep from crying, he turned to the window, where morning sunlight sparkled on snow. Leafless branches of a forsythia bush moved in the wind. Next to the forsythia, twigs of red dogwood stuck up from the snow. Every object out of doors—from the school bus in the driveway to trees by the ball field—seemed unusually clear. And he realized in that instant that everything in the landscape, including light itself, had changed. It was a new world. The plate-glass cage in which he had lived was gone. On a Monday morning a little after eleven o'clock he was free.

FIFTEEN

Invitation

February 3, 1955

Vinnie and Linda Angeleno taught ballroom dancing at schools on Long Island's north shore. Their classes were private, each class starting at three thirty in the afternoon in one or another gymnasium. Crystal Elementary had its class on Thursdays. Despite the fifteen-dollar fee for ten lessons, parents dug deep. Angeleno classes were always full.

Part of it had to do with Angeleno charisma. The couple told parents they'd studied fox trot in London with the famous Irene Castle, and had won a silver trophy in New York during United States Amateur Ballroom Dance Competition. But that wasn't all. Maria, an attractive woman with a penchant for diamond tiaras, promoted dance passionately.

"It's as important to success," she said, "as right clothes and a college degree."

Classes at Crystal Elementary began after Christmas and ended in late winter with Dance Competition Night. On the first Thursday in February, Maria discussed Competition Night.

"It will be different this year. As you know, Vinnie and I always choose the dance. Last year we picked the fox trot. In fifty-three it was the Lindy, before that, mambo. This year I've written the names of seven dances on seven snippets of paper. I'll pick the winner from Vinnie's hat."

On cue, Vinnie stepped forward, his socks a white flash between black shoes and pants the same color. Upside down in his hand was a black chauffeur's cap, the same cap he pulled onto his head late every Thursday afternoon when he and Linda Angeleno—with sheet music and a portable record player—exited the gym.

He put in the cap seven bits of paper, each one noting a dance and corresponding musical piece. Linda reached into the hat and, pausing dramatically, lifted a folded paper.

"Another thing," she said, turning to face the milling students. "There will be a prize this year for the winning couple: a gift certificate for an Alfred's Drug Banana Barge."

They all knew what *that* was. Larger than a banana split, the Barge had four scoops of ice cream, chocolate chips, and cherry syrup. It took a foot-long container to hold a Barge.

"Garbage Barge is a more appropriate name," Katherine Kimberly muttered. "I plan to have measles on Competition Night."

Then it turned quiet as Linda unfolded the paper.

"A waltz! 'Invitation to the Dance'! You'll know the number inside out by the end of the month. We'll practice on Thursdays, of course. And you can practice at home. Remember: Winning couple splits the Barge."

The following day after school, sitting on a hay bale together watching the Reds, Jenny talked about the contest.

"My mom's a dancer," she explained. "She'll teach us. She'll show us moves none of the others know. I talked with her already and Dad has 'Invitation' on a record. We'll watch Mom and Dad dance. Then *we'll* do it. And we'll win. Simple as that."

Saying no was impossible. So three hours later, after a mostly word-less supper with Lena and George, Paul went down the snowy Laurel Path in the dark. Minutes later he walked into the Morans' yellow-painted den—"the rumpus room," Bill Moran called it.

Bill sat on the edge of a gray stuffed chair, chin in his hands, leaning over the hi-fi speaker.

"Your dance teachers picked a fine piece of music," he said to Paul. "The composer—Carl Maria von Weber—wrote it for the piano. But 'Invitation to the Dance' is more often played as an orchestral piece."

With her husband as partner, Barbara Moran showed them how Jenny's right hand was to rest lightly in Paul's left, and how Paul was to encircle her waist just so with his right hand.

"The basic move is the box step that you two know by heart: forward, back. Hands and arms in fixed position."

Barbara and Bill Moran danced the forward and back and broke to the open position with bodies parallel, inside hands joined just so. When they were done, smiling and pleased with their demonstration, Barbara had Paul and Jenny try the routine.

It didn't go well for Paul.

Encircling Jenny's waist with his right hand—rumpus room lights glaring above and Jenny's parents three feet away—he was ill at ease. Jenny's dress, the red one she planned to wear on Competition Night, was cinched so tight at the middle that it felt as if he were touching bare flesh. And he couldn't take his eyes from her face—red lips, happy brown eyes, hair swaying. Entranced, he stepped on her toes.

"Paul, Paul," Barbara interrupted, laughing as she walked between the two of them. "You need to listen to the music…"

She paused midsentence. "And stop watching her. Yes, she's beautiful. We think so too. And she's going to be around a long time, Paul. She's not going to disappear. So listen to the music. Think about the dance."

In the next hour, they mastered the formal coquettish bow that begins Weber's "Invitation." They learned the open position and the more difficult reverse. They were still dancing at nine thirty when Barbara, blue jacket draped over her shoulders, excused herself to put the car in the garage. Returning to the house, yellow light from the den window caught her attention, and she stood watching the children glide and turn. She noticed the smile on her daughter's face, and Paul's more serious expression. How good the two of them looked. How well they danced! And they had two more weeks to practice.

On Dance Competition Night, ceiling lights in the gym were dimmed. White streamers hung from the ceiling. A makeshift chandelier, rigged by the Crystal Elementary janitor, cast a circle of light on the floor. Parents sat in folding chairs along a wall, cigarettes glowing like fireflies.

At exactly seven thirty, Linda Angeleno, wearing a red sequined dress, green heels clicking on the gym floor, walked to the center of the room. With fingers of two hands clasped fanlike to her chest, she explained the rules of the dance. Paul and Jenny stood motionless, as did the competition: Kate Donaldson with David Edgar, Sandy Bartlett with Donald Jones, and—smiling—Brenda and Owen. Katherine Kimberly, despite her pledge to come down with measles, stood by her partner, David Bean.

With the first opening chords of "Invitation," every couple but one began gliding about the gym. Paul and Jenny stood in place seconds longer to make their introductory bows, Jenny turning away from her partner momentarily the way Barbara Moran had demonstrated. *Coquettish* was the word Barbara had used to describe the right way to begin "Invitation."

Then they moved to the music, Jenny's right hand in Paul's left, his right hand lightly at her waist guiding her. Soon they stopped counting steps and thinking about what came next because everything was familiar from practice in the rumpus room, and all they had to do was listen to the ebb and flow of the "Invitation." Their eyes met as the music quickened, and they smiled. It was going well.

Open. Reverse. Forward. Cuddle. Open. Faster and faster they went. At the periphery of their vision they saw the Angelenos moving among the dancers, tapping one couple after another until only Brenda and Owen remained, and Paul was careful to guide Jenny around so there would be no collision in spite of how fast they whirled. Then Paul and Jenny were alone on the floor, dancing around and around, ignoring the clapping and whistles as they listened for the final movement that signaled ending bows. Applause sounded through the gym.

But Vinnie had "Invitation" going a second time, and they saw from Linda's nod that they were to dance an encore.

When it was finally over, the clapping died away, and the certificate for the free Banana Barge was presented, Paul saw—walking out of the darkness—his old teacher, Miss Rita Hart. He assumed she was coming to congratulate Jenny because Miss Hart liked her. But when Miss Hart drew close, she stopped in front of him.

"You two were beautiful," she said, her eyes meeting his. "Beautiful. I am so happy Paul that…that everything is going well for you."

She patted his shoulder and, smiling at Jenny, turned and walked away. And suddenly Paul was aware that all of the time Rita Hart had been speaking, and before that—during applause and presentation of the Banana Barge certificate—he had held Jenny's hand. And still they held hands.

100

SIXTEEN
Alone

March 13, 1955

It was day two of spring vacation, and Paul took the Laurel Path to Jenny's. Whatever Jenny wanted to do that day—be it cleaning the chicken house or reading indoors—he'd join her.

At the bottom of the path, footing slushy with melting snow, the first person he saw was Bill Moran.

He was bolting a ski rack to the Oldsmobile roof.

Then Paul spotted Jenny on the porch.

"You're here!" she yelled, her ski boots in one hand and a suitcase in the other. "I was about to phone you. Can you take care of the Reds while I'm away? And feed my fish? You're the only one I trust."

Seeing his hangdog look, she dropped boots and suitcase in a pile and ran to him.

"This is my dad's Christmas present to the family: six days of spring skiing at Cannon Mountain in New Hampshire. Mom and I didn't know when. Then Dad told us—popped it on us, I should say—over breakfast. She glanced at her father, at that moment lifting suitcases into his car's trunk.

"You know how my dad is about the North Country. That's his name for the place. *North Country.* Now don't turn grumpy on me. Skiing up there is fun. Better than our Wilhoite Pond disaster, at any rate. And I'm sorry I couldn't tell you earlier."

Jenny leaned close, tugging his jacket collar.

"Hey. Shape up. We'll eat the damn Garbage Barge next week."

Paul stood in the driveway until the white Olds disappeared down Sylvan Road. Then he slouched up the path toward home.

What would he do for the next six days?

Suddenly he stopped. It was Sunday, after all. He'd visit David.

Breaking into a run, he vaulted onto the kitchen steps, kicked off his boots, and clomped upstairs for the Argus.

Ten minutes later, camera slung from his shoulder, he reached the Steins' front door. Blue smoke rose from the chimney. That was a good sign, Paul thought. David was surely home…

But he wasn't.

"He's in East Hampton," Rachel said, holding the door for Paul. "He's doing a four-day photo shoot at Jackson Pollock's house. He's a big-name artist in New York, and his show at the Met opens in April. David learned about the assignment just last night.

"But come in. I have bran muffins hot from the oven."

"I can't, Rachel. I'm going to the West Hills. It's a long ways away. I need to start now."

Paul did intend to photograph the West Hills. That much was true. He'd thought about it for weeks. But he'd had no plan to hike there today—not before learning that David, like Jenny, had evaporated from Crystal.

Now he wanted to be alone; alone to think and sulk and walk until he was too tired to hurt.

"Okay," Rachel said. "Just leave yourself time to get back. It's dark by six-thirty."

Between the Steins' house and Jayne's Hill—highest point on the West Hills ridge—lay mile-long Oak Dale Forest, followed by the hundred-acre Wykoff Potato Farm. Dead reckoning got Paul through the forest. And his spirit improved as he tramped across the Wykoff field, its fall-sown winter rye already green. The trail up Jayne's Hill was pleasant too, sun warm on his back and the going easy.

But when he stood on the round-topped summit overlooking gray Long Island Sound and the distant Connecticut hills, his mood darkened. North of those hills, he knew, Jenny would soon be skiing. In his imagination, he pictured a high school boy at her side. Perhaps she would smile at him, head to one side, the way she smiled at *him*.

Paul looked down at the muddy summit of Jayne's Hill and—without taking a single photograph—left the ridge.

At home in his bedroom by six-thirty that night, he studied Jenny's dark house through the west window. When the lights flashed on, he was joyful for a second. Then he guessed the truth. Bill Moran had the house lights on a timer.

*　　*　　*

At eight o'clock the next morning, Lena Howland answered the ringing phone.

"Yes," she said. "You have the right number."

Left hand pressed to the receiver, she motioned to Paul just coming downstairs.

"Mike Britain? You know a Mike Britain?"

Paul nodded as he took the receiver. Mike was the *Mirror* feature editor. They'd spoken last August when Paul took pictures for the vanishing farm story.

"Good to find you in town! Once again we need your help," the editor said, his fast-clip voice spewing out particulars.

"We're in a pickle here because our beat-assigned photogs are all in the boroughs, and David's off to the Hamptons. What I'm looking for is someone to shoot pics for a 'Winter Baymen' story I've planned for months. Problem is, we're running out of winter. Spring starts the twenty-first. So the story's got to run Sunday. I'd like to use it page one in the Long Island edition. Can you do it?"

"Yes."

"Terrific. Lucky for you, our mutual friend Clyde Benson's a boater. I've reserved a fourteen-foot skiff and outboard for the two of you at Milt's Evinrude next to Clam Shack Row. That's the south end of Blue Water Harbor."

Paul knew the place well. Twice he'd rowed there with Jenny.

"You'll meet your clammers three o'clock tomorrow on the beach by Clam Shack Row. They're sure to be there getting boats ready for the evening tide. Follow them to the clam beds. Clyde can interview from the stern. You shoot from the bow."

So the next day, Paul rode with Clyde to Clam Shack Row, the closed-for-winter shacks looking drab and peel-painted in the afternoon light.

On a pebbly strand by the shacks, a young bayman carried twelve-foot clam tongs and a bushel measure to his open boat. A second digger caught Paul's attention: an old man at that moment pushing his boat toward open water. Paul joined him at the stern and—with two pushing—the boat slid quickly to the low-tide line.

Despite the help, the old man shook his head when he learned why the strangers had come to Clam Shack Row.

"I'm sorry, given that you helped me push this crate. But I got no time, kid. Look at my hands. Swollen to hell. That's arthritis and blistered frostbite. It takes me twice the time as that young fella there just to get a bushel of cherrystone. That's six dollars for an evening's work. And if it's a chowder bed my tongs hit, I make two dollars on a bushel. You get what I'm saying, kid? I work slow. No time for pictures."

From fifteen feet away, the younger bayman shouted to Paul.

"Name's Roy Stump. Call me Stumpy like everyone else. Muff Driscoll there's telling you true. Nice guy. Just hurting a lot these days. Muff likes to work alone, but clams with me for his safety. Anyway, take my picture if you want. When my girlfriend sees it in the *Mirror*, she just might, ah…be nice to me."

Blue Water Harbor was calm six feet above the bed of hard-shells. With their boats anchored offshore, the men worked their scissor-like tongs standing up. Clyde cut the outboard to interview Roy Stump. Paul made a dozen quick shots: the digger's face and straining arms, mud-black clams in the tongs, Roy's gray boat in sun-flecked water.

When the skiff drifted right and hit Muff Driscoll's boat, Paul feared the bayman's anger.

He didn't have to.

"You newspaper fellas brought the luck with you," the old clammer said. "Looky here—nearly a bushel of cherrystone and hardly an hour on the water. Take what pictures you want. You'll get no guff from me."

The calm salt water, the man's genial response—the sun just then setting—all conspired to put Paul in a mood to experiment. Reaching for his canvas bag, he grasped a flashgun and pushed it onto the camera's hot shoe. He popped a bulb into the unit and set his lens to its smallest aperture, f-22. Then he stood to make his portrait of the clammer, Argus lens pointed into the sun that peeked from behind the old man's shoulder.

"All I see is blue dots," Muff Driscoll said.

It was near dark when the three boats returned to Clam Shack Row.

Sitting in the stern of the beached skiff, Paul wrote captions on a sheet of copy paper borrowed from Clyde. He folded it small and stuffed it in the Kodak film box with the exposed film.

"I'll guard it with my life," Clyde said. "Mike will see it on his desk first thing tomorrow."

Wednesday morning, Mike called.

"This is a day to remember. I got a Benson story before deadline and five good pics from you, among them a winner that will knock the socks off readers. It's your shot of the old man, Muff Driscoll. You see his scarred hands in the picture, white hair down to his eyes. Then above his shoulder there's a sunburst with radial lines. How in hell did you make that happen?"

"Small aperture with fill flash, Mr. Britain. And luck."

"Hold onto the luck, Paul. We need it."

Four boring days later, tire sounds next door alerted Paul to the Oldsmobile's arrival. He ran so fast down the Laurel Path that the car doors were hardly open when he reached his neighbors' drive. Jenny, struggling to remove skis from the roof rack, didn't see him at first. He called her name and reached for her hand.

"I missed you," he said. She pulled back, glancing toward her mother. From Barbara's grin, it was clear she'd seen it all.

"Help me get these things off the car, Paul," Jenny ordered, hammering the skis with her fists. "They're still frozen to the damn rack. That's how cold it is up there."

Using the pointed end of a ski pole, Paul chipped away, careful not to scratch the car.

Later, as he lugged the last suitcase to the house, Jenny caught up with him, ski boots dangling from laces wound about her wrist. Peering left and right to be sure no one watched, she bumped him hard with her hip.

"I missed you too. How are the Rhode Island Reds?"

SEVENTEEN

Change

"You can change your mind. I haven't told the Eagle."

Eagle was Mike Britain's nickname for Everett Golden, publisher of the *New York Mirror*.

Golden's office and clerical staff filled the top floor of the Flatiron Building, headquarters for Golden & Golden since 1921.

In Mike's office four floors down, a rattling air conditioner did little to relieve discomfort from the season's first heat wave. It was five in the afternoon. Except for the front page and its jump, the morning paper was "put to bed," an expression Mike used when responsibility for getting out the next day's paper switched from his desk to the basement pressroom.

Across from Britain's desk, David Stein leaned back in a swivel chair.

"I appreciate it, Mike. Appreciate your holding off. But no. Tell the Eagle. My first day at the *East Hampton Star* is July eighteenth."

"What I don't get, David, is why? You'll make two-thirds of what you earn here, and from what you've told me, that house you're buying—raccoons in the basement and bats upstairs—isn't something to write home about. Yeah, I know you're tired of car wrecks and murders. But they go with the territory, for Christ's sake. And come to think of it, you haven't shot a crime scene in more than a month. Last one I recall is the Bedford-Stuyvesant thing last May."

"Wrong. You were off Saturday night. That's when the nut in Queens strung up his wife from a water pipe. I was there."

For a moment, neither spoke. David swiveled. The AC rattled.

"Have you told Paul?" Mike asked. "What's his take on your leaving Crystal?"

David looked at the floor. "Haven't told him yet."

Mike shook his head. "Not fair keeping him in the dark. The kid worships you. My biggest fear, if you want to know the truth, is that Paul will quit freelancing when you're out of the picture. Think of where that puts me. My best New York photographer runs off to the *Star*, and I stand to lose my best shooter on the Island."

That night David arranged a Sunday morning photo excursion with Paul. Three days later they tramped the oak and laurel forest beyond the Steins' house. When David suggested they continue to Jayne's Hill, Paul shrugged.

"We can. But I've been there. I climbed the ridge in March when Jenny went skiing and you'd gone to photograph the artist. There's a good view from the summit. But you need a telephoto lens to get a winner. Long Island Sound and Connecticut are too far away for the fifty-millimeter stuff we're carrying."

So they canceled the Jayne's Hill plan and walked instead to the end of Oak Dale Forest. There they sat on big round stones facing the Wykoff Potato Farm. Before them, rows of white-blossomed potato plants spread toward the horizon.

And David told Paul about leaving.

"Why?" the boy asked, repeating the question Mike Britain had raised days earlier.

David pointed to the west edge of the farm.

"See that? See those red flags at the woods line? I count twenty-five."

He paused.

"Each flag marks a house site. They'll be framed in by summer's end. By Thanksgiving, families from the city will be dickering over prices with the developer. Next year there'll be another line of flags. Then more, until there's no more potato farm. That's what's happening to this end of the Island. That's part of why we're leaving.

"There are things I'll miss about Crystal: beaches, Blue Water Harbor, Sylvan Road on a winter morning. And there are things about this place I won't t miss one bit, like that Swimmers' Club next to Clam Shell Beach. Did I tell you what they did to us?

"You know how much Rachel likes to swim, right? How Rachel is about her exercise? Well, last year I decided to join their little club so Rachel could swim laps even in winter. Their pool is Olympic-size and open all year. You have to apply to join, and applicants need a sponsor who's already a member. Your girlfriend's father, Bill Moran, sponsored us. He wrote the club a corker of a letter about Rachel and me. I know because he gave me a carbon copy.

"So I mailed in the application. Then we waited. And waited. Six months passed and still no word. Mind you, we'd mailed the application in November and here it was practically summer already. So I called the Swimmers' Club and asked about the hold-up. Turns out they rejected us the same week we applied—and didn't bother to inform us. I lost my temper with this lady on the phone, and she hung up. Of course I know why they turned us down."

The sun was pleasantly warm. Before them, the West Hills ridge had the blue cast of higher mountains.

"Beautiful," David said at length. "But there's a nastiness about this place, Paul. Crystal is like *Beauty and the Beast.* The beast part gives me the creeps."

They talked photography on the walk home. David was cautiously pleased. Paul had taken it well. He was on his path. And the *Mirror* connection through Mike Britain would help him over the bump.

Indeed, Paul wasn't devastated. Later that day, lunching on bagels and cream cheese in Rachel's kitchen, the couple invited him for a week-long stay in East Hampton. "Mid-August," said David. "The ocean's beautiful then. You'll have new territory to photograph and seven days of Rachel's good cooking. Best of all, your father's already given the okay!"

The impact of David's departure was further softened by an unexpected happening: Jenny and Paul's first double date. It was Jenny's idea. Her mother, encouraging from the start, agreed to chauffeur and make phone calls. The event was an afternoon showing of the Nunnally Johnson movie, *The Black Widow.* Owen and Brenda comprised the other half of the date.

To make it more interesting, Barbara Moran promised the four they'd stop afterwards at Mickey's Carvel to sample the town's first soft-serve ice cream.

In the packed theater, they found empty seats three rows from the screen. The movie was a murder mystery in which a writer named Peggy

Ann Garner dies—and an innocent man friend is falsely accused.

Craning his neck to watch, Paul was mesmerized by the movie's sweeping cinemascope photography of New York City. Filmed from terraces in skyscraper apartments, he saw magic in the Technicolor views of busy streets below. Oh, to bring his Argus to the city, he thought—to look down through its lens from the top of the Empire State Building! What amazing possibilities lay close by!

There was something else about the movie just as exciting. High in the empty apartment where she writes, Peggy Ann Garner listens repeatedly to a recording of the opera *Salome* with its haunting refrain: *The mystery of love is greater than the mystery of death.*

Was there ever a sentiment more romantic? Careful not to startle her, Paul wrapped his arm about the hard wooden back of Jenny's seat.

Later, Barbara Moran held the car door as the four of them piled into the backseat. Any tension felt at the start of this first double date disappeared on the ride home from Mickey's Carvel.

"I got a new bathing suit yesterday," Brenda announced. "White with red polka dots. I'll wear it when we go to the beach tomorrow. If I dare. It's skimpy."

"Skimpy's good," Owen said.

"I'll pretend I didn't hear that," she said, stifling giggles.

In the car mirror, Barbara Moran watched—and smiled.

"Brenda," she said, catching the girl's eye, "do you remember years ago driving with us to Hanna Abelson's party? You were seven then, maybe eight. You sat for the longest time looking at your red boots without saying one word: a beautiful silent girl with long, long hair. You seem so much happier now, Brenda. How come?"

The girl looked to the mirror. She'd always liked Barbara Moran—the rides to birthday parties, drives to the beach. There was something between the two of them, she thought. An understanding. Something of that sort.

"I love Mrs. Christy," she said, meeting Barbara's eyes in the mirror. "She invited me to her house in the winter. We had tea on her porch. She showed me a porcelain doll she's had since she was a little girl. It had teeth. Little sharp teeth. When I left, she gave me a book about dolls and doll collecting."

Silent for a moment, Brenda turned from the mirror to glance at the rush of green trees by the roadside.

"I'm going to be a teacher when I grow up. A teacher like Mrs. Christy. The kind that helps kids."

EIGHTEEN

Passing

July 16, 1955

"The McLean woman's dead."

It was Saturday. George Howland, *Crystal Gazette* spread on the kitchen table, read aloud to Lena. "'Born July 12, 1873, she was the youngest child of James and Sarah Tallman. An older sister, Miriam, died in 1949. Mrs. McLean attended a one-room schoolhouse before graduating from Whitman Normal School in 1893.'"

"No spring chicken," Lena said. "Now Ross, her husband—he was a sketch. Ross I liked. And how long has he been dead?"

George, ignoring her question, pushed away the *Gazette*.

"You can bet they'll be scuffling over that piece of real estate. Bob Lyford's probably on the phone now trying to get his three acres. But that McLean heir, Peter Something-or-other, he'll sell the farm intact to a bigwig developer from Manhattan. Mark my words."

Paul, pausing on the stairs, listened. Minutes earlier, he'd wound a roll of Plus-X into the Argus, intending to photograph the very farm his parents had just discussed.

Now he headed for Jenny's.

On the Laurel Path, he tried to think of Mary, now gone forever— her house closed up and musty, the pastures growing to weeds. But his thoughts skipped to Jenny. What was wrong with her the last couple of weeks? When he suggested walking the railroad tracks, she refused. She didn't want to swim. Bicycling to the fish hatchery bored her. Uncertainty nipped at the edge of his mind. Had Jenny grown tired of him? Had she fallen in love with another boy?

But five minutes later, when he found her at the Rhode Island Red pen, she was more like herself. They talked about Mary.

"I've been thinking," Jenny said, pulling a handful of leaves from a birch, then stuffing them through the wire to the hens. "Thinking how different my life would be if I'd been born in 1873 instead of 1941. I decided I'd be happier living in Mary's time. You had to work harder then. But there was less heartbreak."

She suggested they sail the Lightning.

Half an hour later, she stood on the deck in her blue one-piece bathing suit, pushing a wooden stay into the boat's mainsail. Paul fixed the tiller to the stern and, when he'd run the mainsail out along the boom, Jenny cast off the red mooring. For a second, the boat drifted. Then wind caught its sail and *Art Spirit* heeled to port.

It was easy holding the sailboat on a good tack, and when he smiled at Jenny sitting cross-legged in the bow, he knew she was happy. For an hour they tacked across Blue Water Harbor, the rippling sound of little waves slapping the boat's hull.

But the wind died a mile from the mooring. Paul took down the mainsail. At the bow point, legs port and starboard, Jenny paddled. The boat hardly moved.

"Stop playing with the damn sails. Help me!"

He came forward. She moved to one side, and they paddled together in the bow as *Art Spirit* headed in.

"I wasn't playing, Grouch. I was stowing sail. Making your mom's boat shipshape."

Twenty minutes later, Paul tied the Lightning to its buoy. Jenny dove from the bow as he worked, splashing him deliberately. Two feet away she surfaced, strands of wet hair down her cheeks.

She spit water in his face.

"S-or-r-r-r-y."

Paul tumbled over the side in a cannonball, hearing her squeal as he hit the water.

Then he rowed the pram toward shore while Jenny dripped in the stern.

"Hot out here," he said. "Tide's low."

A long pier separated Clam Shell Beach from the Swimmer's Club. Instead of rowing to a spit of sand east of the dock—a place where they usually tied the dinghy—Paul pulled the port oar hard. The boat bounced lightly against barnacle-crusted pilings and glided beneath the pier. It was green-dark there and cool as a cave. He decided to kiss Jenny.

After all, they'd kissed before.

Beyond the dock, somewhere out in the glaring sun, an outboard whined. They turned and saw Johnny Verstaces's thirty-horse runabout circling closer. Johnny was a sophomore at Crystal High. He knew where they were. But in the shade of the dock, small waves lapping against pilings, who cared about Johnny Verstaces? Paul grasped the gunwales. Leaning close, he touched her body wet from swimming. Strands of hair clung to her neck.

She drew away.

"Stop it," she said, pushing him away. "We're moving. August twenty-sixth. My dad's opened a practice in Plainfield."

Stunned, Paul gripped the gunwales harder. The whine of Johnny Verstaces outboard grew loud, yet he paid no attention as the meaning of Jenny's words came clear.

"You can't!" he shouted. "You've got the Rhode Island Reds. Your turtle with the broken shell. And we're going to Crystal High. Together."

She screamed and lunged for his hands as the speedboat appeared in blazing sun mere feet from the dock, Johnny slamming its stern ninety degrees to port so a four-foot wake hit the dinghy broadside.

"Your hands! Your hands!"

She grasped Paul's bloody arm and pulled while he clung to the little boat as it rose and fell against knife-sharp barnacles.

In white light four feet from the dock, Johnny Verstaces looked ashen-faced at the two of them. He jammed the runabout throttle forward and the boat, stern digging low in the water, sped to the center of the harbor.

When the last wave coursed through the pilings and the pram floated calm, Jenny dropped to her knees in the stern of the boat, cradling Paul's hands. "You idiot. How stupid of you," she said; her voice kind in spite of her scolding.

And she held his injured hands as salt water and blood ran down her forearms to pool in the dinghy's bilge.

"Move your fingers," she ordered.

He yanked his hands away, furious with her for playing nurse, for calling him stupid—and for going away forever.

"It's a barnacle cut. Barnacle cuts bleed. Leave me alone."

When Barbara Moran met them at the beach, she went to Paul. She held his arm gently, examining his wrist and fingers.

"It's a barnacle cut," he said, anticipating her question.

He rode home in the backseat, a white towel around his wrist. He watched trees as the towel turned red.

*　*　*

On July thirtieth, Dr. Peter Graham removed all but a small piece of bandage on Paul's knuckles. Whistling as he tossed the gauze into a wastebasket, he announced cheerfully that "good old penicillin did the trick again."

Paul wanted to believe that Jenny was not leaving. Her father had made a bad decision, he reasoned. Bill would change his mind. Some mornings, Paul lay in bed imagining Jenny's eager knock on the kitchen door and her happy shout: *We're staying on the Island!*

But holding his daydream proved impossible. Workmen hammered a FOR SALE sign into Jenny's lawn. A larger sign—PRIME ONE-ACRE LOTS—appeared in Mary's field.

NINETEEN

Interlude

August 13, 1955

George Howland, eating French toast when Paul came into the kitchen, raised his index finger.

"Mr. Stein called last night and invited you to the Hamptons. I nixed the idea. But your mother overruled. The upshot is, you'll leave Monday for a week. I'll put you on the train at Crystal Station. You'll backtrack to Jamaica, then ride the South Shore line to the Hamptons."

It was bad news for Paul. Jenny was due to leave August twenty-sixth, and he'd counted on being with her for thirteen more days. Now they'd be together just four. But as he thought more about David's offer, the vacation from Crystal had some appeal. Jenny was grouchy lately. So was he. A few days' separation might be a good thing.

So Monday morning he boarded the crowded railway car at Crystal Station. Four hours later, David jumped partway onto the train to clap Paul on the shoulders. He reached for the boy's suitcase, noticing Paul's injured hand as he did.

"Holy cow! What happened there?"

"It's a barnacle cut," Paul told him, opening and closing his fist to show that everything worked. "It looks bad, but it's pretty much all better. Where's Rachel?"

"Home," David said, loping along the wooden-plank train platform, Paul's suitcase swinging from his arm. "Getting our supper ready, even if it's six hours away. You know Rachel. She had me go to Overton's Fish Pound this morning for halibut, then to Sag Harbor for everything else she needs for gefilte fish. Now don't let her know I told. She wants it to be a surprise."

They bounced out of the rutted station lot in David's gray Plymouth, the car hot from standing in the sun. For a while they drove in shade between rows of elms. The trees ended where the road passed a dairy farm. It reminded Paul of Mary McLean's place, though the East Hampton farm was anything but deserted. Holstein cows grazed by the road. In the distance, a red hay baler pulled by a tractor expelled yellow cubes of hay.

Then the road narrowed as it entered shady woodland, tree branches forming a bridge of leaves above. Driving with all windows open, wind distorting his voice, David told Paul about his work at the *Star*: portraits he made of fishermen, coves he photographed at sunrise, artists he'd introduce to Paul.

"The light's incredible here. Intense. White. Must be the nearness of ocean or open farmland."

David talked more about East Hampton—how the ocean hammered the shore, the calm water of Accabonic Creek a stone's throw from Fireplace Road where he and Rachel were trying to reclaim their house from a family of raccoons.

For the first time since Jenny's sad news, Paul felt happy. The photographer's excitement buoyed his spirit.

David swung the Plymouth sharp left down a narrow gravel driveway, braking to a stop by a small shingle-style house baked white by the sun.

Rachel threw open the front screen door, which slammed shut as she ran to hug Paul.

"You're hand!" she cried, her arms still wrapped around him. "What happened?"

"Don't worry," David said. "Already the boy told me. He has a barnacle cut. Nothing to worry about."

They ate lunch at a table next to a cot on the porch. Beyond the porch was a field of sun-bleached grass.

Off and on, despite the new landscape and Rachel's animated chatter, thoughts of Jenny pushed into Paul's mind. How could he live without her day after day? How slowly time would pass without her.

"Hey, Paul," Rachel said. "Listen up! Come back from the planets! We're going to the ocean. You'll love it."

Half an hour later, Paul stood waist-deep in pounding white surf. Green waves swirling about were colder—much colder—than the slack warm water at Clam Shell Beach. He looked over his shoulder to the white sand beach where Rachel and David sat chatting. Then he dove headfirst through the breakers and swam until he was tired.

He turned back toward land and treaded water. People on the shore appeared small as dolls.

How Jenny would love it here, he thought. She would surface and dive, the two of them moving like fish in the cold green ocean. But they would never be here together.

Despite numbing cold, he swam farther from shore. And what would it be like, he wondered, if he went on swimming?

After a while, he concluded, the discomfort of cold would go away. By then it would be too late to regain the beach.

At that moment he decided to go back. But he swam slowly now. When he stopped to tread water again, he saw a commotion on shore. A lifeguard ran toward the ocean, red surfboard clutched across his chest. Much closer, a swimmer cut through the water, her eyes locked on his. It was Rachel.

Hours later, wolfing gefilte fish in the warm cottage, he tried to recall the sequence of his rescue. He remembered Rachel grabbing his hair. And the lifeguard, Ed, sliding him onto the surfboard. Then came nonsense recollections that ended when he opened his eyes on the beach, army blankets heavy on his chest. He sat bolt upright in time to see an ambulance and police car depart down the dusty beach road.

"You scared us, you miserable termite," he remembered David saying.

No one mentioned his near drowning until midway through dinner when Rachel, placing her knife and fork at the edge of her plate, leaned across the table.

"So why did you go out there? You were four hundred feet offshore. That's longer than a football field, Paul. The water is sixty-one degrees. Did you think you'd just swim back? Or...was there something else you had in mind?"

He was tired. Still, he'd expected the question.

"I did it for fun," he said. "To see how far out I could swim. I didn't realize how cold I'd get. I'm sorry I caused such a mess. Thank you for rescuing me, Rachel."

His cot on the porch was harder than his bed at home. He lay on his back, fingers clasped beneath his head. Water sounds from a dishwasher mingled with David and Rachel's talk in the kitchen. Through the porch screen, he watched a rectangle of sky change from amber-blue to black. Stars appeared.

He thought of Jenny, remembering the ski trip that had taken her away for seven days. He had six more days in the Hamptons.

Turning away from the stars, he closed his eyes. An hour later, he fell into a troubled sleep, dreaming that he was at the high-tide line on Clam Shell Beach. Down by the water's edge, Jenny raised the Lightning's sail. They were leaving together. But when Paul tried to join her, a blast of off-shore wind filled the Lightning's sail, throwing the boom to a long reach that pushed the boat into a sea that changed in Paul's dream from placid Blue Water Harbor to churning green ocean. He had to reach Jenny, yet froze to the beach as she struggled and shrieked, her desolate screams loud in his ears.

He sat up. Awake. Alert. And still the screams went on. Silence finally came when gray light of morning filled the sky.

"Night hawks," David said, putting his coffee cup noisily onto the table. "They hang out at the end of our driveway by the streetlight. Catching moths, I imagine."

Minutes later, a bowl of Cheerios balanced on his lap, Paul sat beside David as the Plymouth bumped down the gravel drive and turned onto Fireplace Road. Fog, rising evenly through the still air, formed a flattened cloud two feet above the car.

"What you shooting?" David asked.

"Kodak Tri-X. First time, too." He'd read about the new film in *Popular Photography*.

"Good choice," David said, slapping the steering wheel. "The fog's burning off. Tide's out. Wait until you see this gem of a beach between Wainscot and West End Road."

It was as good as David promised: dunes thick with blue-green grass, white sand below the dunes, and a tidal plain that stretched from high on the beach down to white surf falling rhythmically against rocks. Wet and luminous, the tidal zone was a mirror reflecting sky and clouds.

"I'm shooting in the dunes. I've done the reflection before," David told him as he climbed the first sand bank, Speed Graphic cradled in his arms.

Sitting on a boulder, Paul watched the surf. He was tired. He looked at his watch. It was seven forty-five. And what was Jenny doing now? Sleeping, he decided. Morning light soft on her pillow and sheets. Paul put his head in his hands and curled comma-like on the flat stone. David found him there, half asleep and groggy, when he returned from the dunes.

"Heart not in it, I imagine." the photographer said. "You've been through a lot. Dollars to donuts you're missing Jenny, too."

Paul tried to keep back tears and almost succeeded.

"Listen," David said. "Rachel and I are here for the duration. You can visit us anytime. There's a westbound train leaving at nine. You can catch it if we hustle."

A half hour later, they walked three abreast down East Hampton's wide sidewalk, Paul between the adults as they made their way toward the station. Strangers smiled or nodded at David. Already they knew him, Paul thought. He felt proud walking beside the *Star*'s new photographer. Perhaps they thought he was their son.

Three red railway cars, weathered sides splintery and old, seemed out of place behind the new orange-and-black diesel engine that whistled twice, heat waves rising from its flat top. Climbing into the last car, Paul chose a window seat. When the train jerked forward and whistled again, he opened the top half of the window, turning his head sideways to fit through the opening. He waved and hollered good-bye to the receding figures—David shading his eyes from the sun, Rachel looking small and wistful. When they were out of sight, he turned toward the engine where wind from their gathering speed scattered gray diesel smoke against the train. Clapboard houses flashed by the tracks.

Faster and faster they moved, the train swaying as it fairly burst out of woodlands on silver tracks over green potato fields. Red tractors crawled slowly in the distance. Irrigation sprayers turned in slow arcs, sunlight glinting on the spray. Feeling the wind in his hair, aware of the flowing fields and scattered cumulus clouds, Paul entered a state of being where past and future vanish. And there was only the train flowing west over the green Long Island fields, its wonderfully mournful whistle proclaiming itself to the world.

He shuddered when fingers tapped his shoulder. Turning his head and squeezing back into the passenger car, he looked into the not unfriendly eyes of a round-bellied conductor who—standing in the aisle and swaying with the train—pointed to the empty seat. Paul quickly dropped to the straw-colored cushion. Reaching over him, the conductor closed the window. He punched Paul's ticket as the train whistle blew again, the sound wild and sweetly lonesome.

TWENTY

Jenny

August 16, 1955

At two o'clock, half an hour after Lena met Paul at Crystal Station, he rapped hard on the Morans' door. When Jenny appeared—solemn-looking through the screen—she seemed taller and older, her blue short-sleeved blouse tight across her chest.

Aware that he'd stared too long, Paul looked down at his feet as if fascinated by ratty sneakers. When he dared raise his head, there she stood, smiling slyly, nose pressed to the screen.

"Come in!" Bill Moran yelled from the kitchen. He sat on a bench flipping pages of *Life* magazine.

Jenny slid in next to her father, linking her elbow in his. The doctor kissed his daughter on the top of her head. When he turned to Paul, his eyes went to the boy's mostly healed wrist.

"The traveler's back early," he said, pushing the magazine away. "Peter Graham did a good job on that wrist. Still, you'll wear that scar for years. That's the nature of a barnacle abrasion."

When a pot of water boiled on the stove, Bill poured it into the wide top of an hourglass-shaped coffee pot.

Paul was pleased to be back from the Hamptons.

"Let's go to McLean's," he said to Jenny. "We haven't been there since, uh, Mary died."

He would have run for the door—certain Jenny would follow—had it not been for her troubled expression.

"You won't like what they've done there," Bill Moran said, breaking an uncomfortable silence. "We all knew it was coming. But what surprises me is the speed of development. It's like the blitzkrieg."

Through the kitchen window, Paul watched leaf shadows dance on the side of Jenny's red barn. A Rhode Island Red voiced her I've-laid-an-egg cackle.

"I know the place was special to you both."

The doctor reached across the table and put his hand on Paul's arm, careful to avoid the injury.

"Everything changes, Paul. But it's not the end. There's lots of unspoiled country left."

Paul and Jenny set off for the farm never the less. The trail from Jenny's house to McLean's pond was overgrown. Branches slapped. Spider webs brushed coarse and itchy across their faces.

As they walked, Bill Moran's warning cycled through Paul's mind. *Everything changes.* Whatever had happened, McLean's would not be the same.

His mind raced. In ten days the most important person in his world would be two hundred and eighty-two miles away in a town called Plainfield. Woods and fields in Crystal—their playgrounds since kindergarten—were under attack.

They paused on the first wooded ridge above McLean's Farm. There was no view from the ridge in summer. But they stopped there often because it was peaceful and Mary's farm lay straight ahead downhill.

It wasn't peaceful now. Bulldozer noise and the smell of diesel-powered machinery filled the air. As they stood shoulder to shoulder, a dynamite explosion shook the ground. Leaving the ridge, they walked downhill through the woods, stopping again where gnarled branches parted to frame what had been McLean's Pond.

"I came here yesterday with my dad," Jenny said. "We heard the bulldozers at our house. But by the time we got here they'd finished with the pond.

"It's called a sump," she explained. "They built it for drainage. Runoff from rain will flow into that bulldozed-out place where the pond was. Workmen built it to lower what my dad calls the water table. That way, houses near the sump will have dry cellars."

Half full of brown water, the sump was larger than the pond it had

TWENTY-ONE

Departure

August 26, 1955

At the edge of the Howland lawn, where trampled grass met the Laurel Path, an opening in the leaves revealed the van marked *Crystal Movers*. How quickly August twenty-sixth had arrived.

The squeak of a dolly cart drew Paul's attention. Through green leaves, he saw a burly mover pushing the cart. On it rode suitcases piled like pancakes. Paul sighed and turned away. It was the fifth time he'd checked the movers' progress.

His first trip across the lawn had been at seven thirty-five that morning. Now it was four in the afternoon. He would long since have run to Jenny's house—but for the fact that she'd asked him to stay away.

"Tomorrow will be difficult," she'd said, "and I don't want to break down in front of everyone. But I'll come over at five."

A voice close by startled him.

"It's not nice to spy."

Paul turned to see his mother standing on the brick stoop, right hand clutching the brass doorknob. Her left held the white glass.

"I'm not spying," he said. "Just waiting. Jenny's coming over soon."

Lena nodded as she sat carefully on the stoop. He followed her glance when she looked at the blue sky where a full moon—white like a cloud—rose on the eastern horizon.

"It will be cold tonight," she said, "despite the recent heat. That's because we have a full moon. Ross McLean told me that when he used to deliver milk. He predicted weather by the moon and wind direction. And you know what? He was right most of the time. Ross had a saying: 'Full moon in September, cold to remember.' It isn't September yet, of course. But close enough."

Paul was at peace with his mother. It had been that way for months. At times he'd go searching for her. That generally happened after he'd read something interesting, like the *Popular Photography* article on split filtration. He'd find Lena in the study waxing furniture, or in the cellar pulling wet clothes from the Bendix washer, her hands red from household chemicals that accentuating the stove-burn scars. His mother would straighten up when she saw him coming, standing still to listen, wet clothes she intended to hang outside still in their wicker basket.

Years had passed since his mother had slammed his arithmetic book with her fist or wept for fear of what might become of him. She subscribed to the *Mirror* now. With steel scissors, she cut his photographs from the paper and put them in a shoe box by her bed. He liked it when she patted his shoulder as they passed on the stairs, or when she stood on the brick stoop speaking with him as if he were an adult. She was proud of him now, a fact he still found surprising. Just last week he'd overheard her on the phone bragging to Mrs. Lyford about his rank on the verbal section of the Eighth Grade Regents.

"You're going to need new clothes for high school," Lena said. She sipped the last of her gin and water, tossed ice cubes on the lawn, and went indoors.

For the next hour, Paul paced the lawn, listening for sounds from Jenny's house. Then he went indoors and flipped through pages of *Life* magazine, pausing occasionally to read stories.

When he returned to the lawn it was nearly dark, the full moon yellow in the sky.

There was a rustle on the Laurel Path. And there was Jenny.

"You're late," he said.

She shrugged.

"I can't help that. There was more to pack, and this embarrassing thing happened. I'd stuffed the clothes from my top drawer in a cardboard box, and as I handed the box to this moving van guy in the driveway, the bottom fell out. My underwear and bras landed in a pile. I knelt and picked up everything, this fat galoot standing over me all the while watching. I hate creeps."

He was breathing hard now, fists clenched at his side.

"You have problems following directions, Paul. But get this straight. There will be no trips to Plainfield. Not Thanksgiving. Not Christmas. Not while you're living in this house."

George checked his watch. He threw his pruning shears onto the driveway.

"I'm late," he said. "Got to get to the Studebaker place. Grease job and oil change scheduled for ten."

He turned to his son.

"You're hangdog now. But wait until school starts. You'll meet new friends. Girl friends too. In three months you'll find someone else to break your heart."

Paul crossed the driveway and entered the woods. Once out of sight from his father, he ran for the second ridge where close-growing oaks hid the sump and bulldozed earth. What he saw from the hillside was a slice of fence-crossed pasture yellow-green in the sun. And a cascade of memories descended: the two of them searching for spring peepers, Jenny's little-girl face in the viewfinder of the old Box Brownie, Jenny pleading with him not to disturb the box turtle she discovered by the fence. In this very grove they had kissed mere days ago.

He would write Jenny that afternoon. She would write back. For months or maybe years they would exchange letters. But in time fewer letters would arrive. Looking down at the gray leaves, he remembered Jenny's eyes and the lilac scent of her hair. Sooner or later another boy would have her heart.

By his feet lay a twisted log that he lifted and threw with all his strength against a young birch. The log broke and scattered to pieces as he fell to the ground sobbing. Much later—for the sun was high in the sky—he stood up and looked at the birch he'd pummeled with the log. On its trunk was an inch-long wound.

"Sorry, tree," he said aloud. And felt foolish for apologizing to a tree.

He brushed leaves and sticks from his pants. He pulled his T-shirt out of his belt and wiped his eyes, then tucked it into his jeans. And he felt the amethyst stone, and lifted it carefully from his pocket and held it to the sun. It shone white and purple-blue like the sky.

Turning homeward, he pushed the stone deep into his pocket as he walked beneath green leaves of late summer.

Jenny was right, he thought. Things would work out. High school would begin next week, and it would be okay. Algebra would be difficult. But he could do it. Jenny wouldn't be there to help him with English. But he read everything now. In four years, he'd graduate from Crystal High and go to the Student Art League like David. Then he'd do photography for the *Mirror* for a year or two before going to *Life* magazine.

And there in the woods he imagined himself an adult living in a house with green-growing plants and prints by Matisse and Brueghel. In that distant future he would have a wife and child. Of that he was certain, though he could not see their faces. And as he glimpsed his path ahead and imagined the good places it would lead, he felt nevertheless a terrible sadness in his heart. For no matter how successful he became or who he might someday marry, he would never love anyone as he loved Jenny.